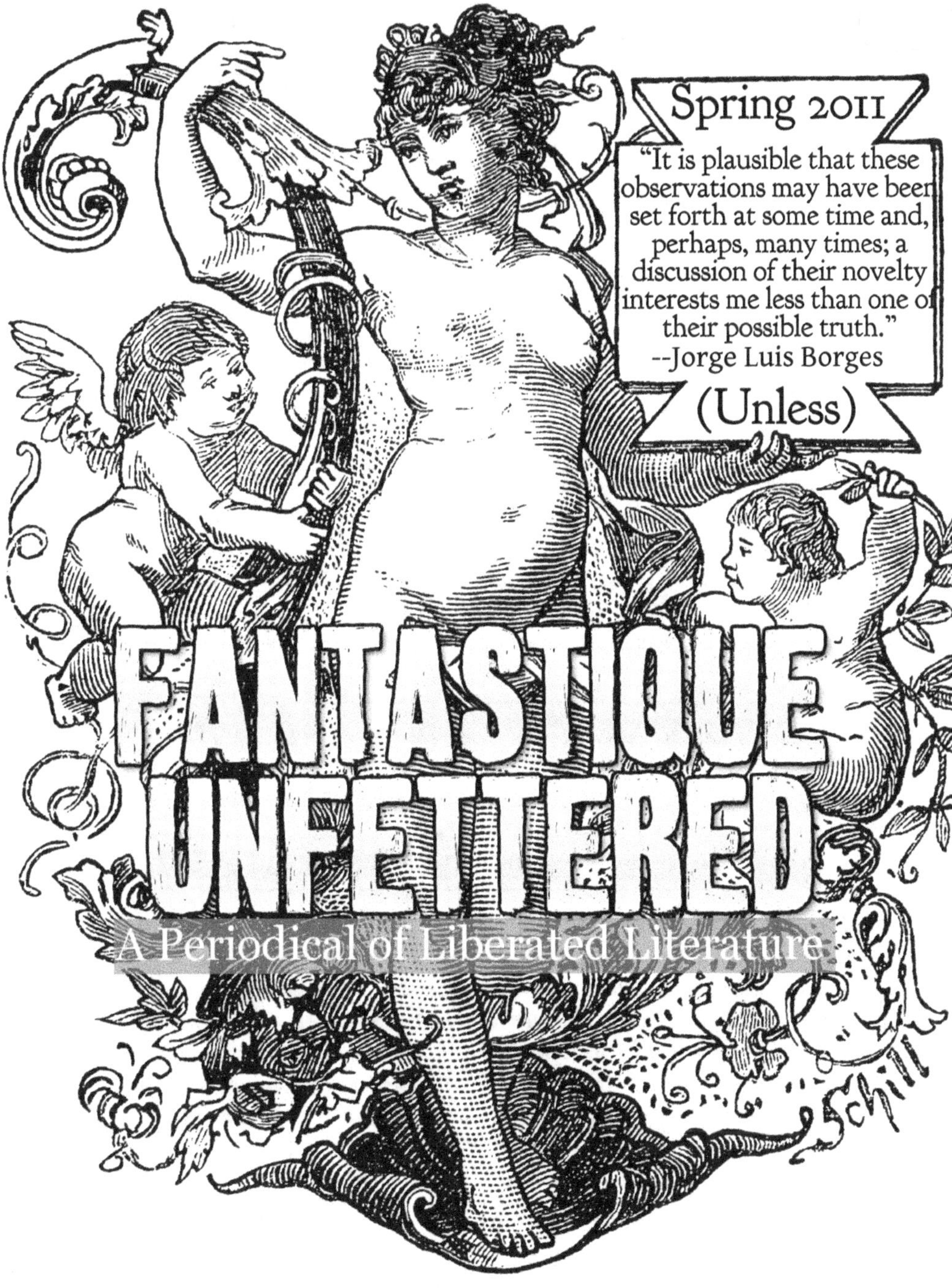
Spring 2011
"It is plausible that these observations may have been set forth at some time and, perhaps, many times; a discussion of their novelty interests me less than one of their possible truth."
--Jorge Luis Borges
(Unless)
FANTASTIQUE UNFETTERED
A Periodical of Liberated Literature
Schill

FANTASTIQUE UNFETTERED

Issue two (Unless) ISBN: 978-0-9831709-2-1

An M-Brane Press Publication

Publisher: Christopher Fletcher

Editor: Brandon H. Bell | Assoc. Editor: Alexandra Seidel | Art & Design Consultant: M. S. Corley | Slush, Editorial Assts.: William Wood, Jaym Gates | Contributing Artists: Luis Beltrán, Mari Kurisato, Chelsea Brandt, and Evan M. Jensen

Fantastique Unfettered is published by M-Brane Press. Send submissions to editors@fantastique-unfettered.com. Find guidelines on the website: www.fantastique-unfettered.com

Some content may not be appropriate for young readers or ideologues. Partake at your own risk.

Suggested retail price is 9.99; actual prices may vary. Order via Amazon, Barnes & Noble, Powells, or anywhere books are sold.
Newstand distribution through Ingram, Baker & Talor, and more.

Credits & attribution: Cover illustration by Luis Beltrán. Cover design by M.S. Corley. FU logo uses the Golden Pony font designed be Ward Zwart. Masthead, Table of Contents, & Contributors list illustrations courtesy oldbookillustrations.com. 'Herein' story rubric, Then Cried Arthur, and end of Bell & Seidel articles illustrations courtesy oldbookart.com. The Kemetian Husesen Craze title page illustration by Mari Kurisato; Dividing Lines and We are Family title page illustrations by Chelsea Brandt. FU#3 teaser cover illustration by Evan M. Jensen. The Aether Age: Helios cover illustration (used in Hail Caesar CC article) is by M.S. Corley.

The Shortest Story...

"Unless," a man once wrote.

Once upon a time, Theodor Seuss Geisel, delivered this message to a pudgy kid with buck teeth and freckles. You matter. You are, in fact, instrumental. Seuss delivered this message to a multitude of children, possibly to you as well.

Something like a story, a diversion intended first and foremost to entertain, might seem a trivial relic best left to childhood, especially in a world filled with strife, hatred, revolution. But kids, the ones already marked by the world as weird or ugly, as Other, know the truth.

Show me a kid that reads, and I'll show you a young lady or young man that cannot be controlled or contained. Not for long.

We are not drones intended only for the accumulation of resources. Ants gathering crumbs. We are gifted, inflicted, with words. While the strong and the powerful squabble over who will rule and who will have, we arrive at the head of a procession of infinite dreams and possibilities, ready to tell or be told the next tale. The one that sticks in our craw or comforts us. The next one that changes everything.

And the dreamers continue in their becoming to arrive among the powerful, the accumulators, the usurpers, to challenge them as well toward something greater than the zero-sum lie that history suggests is our lot. Winners or Losers. The dreamers, stealth bombers with their payloads of nouns and verbs, metaphors and similes, and all manner of weapons of mass construction, arrive to suggest to those who have forgot themselves... A story. A short story. The shortest ever...

"Unless..."

--Brandon H. Bell, April 19th, 2011

Table of Contents

Fiction

Poetry

NonFiction

Every Mother's Child

by
Therese Arkenberg

Herein, a battle cry...

The little girl, Relikin, slept close by me that night, huddled almost in my arms. It didn't do any good; I heard nothing, but by morning she was gone.

I felt like hell, of course, but I wouldn't let myself show it. In the Pit, the ones who seemed to really care went to pieces and then they got taken. That was my theory, at any rate. Joslin told me it seemed to her that the ones who made theories went pretty quickly, too, but she was taken long before me, so screw what she said.

Whatever the reason they took Relikin, I didn't have to dwell on it long, because then I saw something else had changed—someone new had been brought in overnight. A man. The capture had gone hard on him, but I could see he was strong, and probably a warrior, going by the empty scabbard at his belt.

I went to him, picking my way over the prone bodies of the Pit's other prisoners who were still sleeping or had nothing better to do than pretend to sleep. He looked up at my approach, blinking swollen eyelids.

I crouched beside him. "Hey. How're you?"

"Not at my best." He licked his lips, swallowed, then spat blood near my feet. "What the hell were those things?"

I shrugged. "Down here, we call them Pit-keepers."

He looked around, taking in the prone, raggedly-dressed bodies, the stone walls, the pale bluish light from some indistinct source high above. It faded sometimes, in what we called night; that was when people were taken, when the Pit-keepers fed. "I guess this is the Pit?"

"Oh, yeah. Say, my name's Pavadan." Only after I offered my hand did I realize how incongruous the gesture was, but he accepted it.

"Don't... get emotional about things. No matter how much you like your friend, don't smile when you think of him. And don't laugh no matter how funny something is. Never cry."

8

"Rathin." He smiled. Despite the bruises, he wasn't bad-looking. And this close, I could see rolls of muscle through the tears in his shirt. A good choice—I took credit for it, even though it was the Pit-keepers who had chosen, capturing him. I just had the good luck to live long enough to meet him.

"You're a swordsman, aren't you, Rathin?"

"Yeah. How could you—" He looked down and saw his empty scabbard, then his eyes went to my own. "Oh. I see."

"I've been here about three months, near as I can tell. I was part of the hired guard escorting a caravan over the plains. The 'van was attacked—everyone taken. I'm the only one left."

"The only one left?"

"All the others," I said, "are gone. In the night. Nobody ever sees what happens, but down here people...vanish and don't come back."

He pushed himself up, and his bright eyes darted over the Pit. "Was anybody else brought in with me?"

"I don't think so."

"I was traveling with a wizard, a friend of mine. A good friend. We got separated, and when I was looking for him I ran into...Well, you know."

I nodded. I didn't know, exactly, none of us did, but we all agreed: whatever it was had sharp teeth and many claws.

"You don't think..." A frown started, more in the wrinkles of his forehead than around his mouth.

And here was the one man I hoped wouldn't go emotional on me. "Look—whenever they get somebody, they put them down here. If your wizard isn't here—especially after only one night—he's safe."

Rathin relaxed. "Well, that's something."

It was. Perhaps, I realized, someone with strong ties to the outside world, a friend he needed to find, would be even better for my purposes than someone who cared for nothing. "There's something more," I said. "I think I can get us out of here."

That got his attention so fast I expected his eyes to pop from their sockets. "Really? How?"

"I, ah..." I scratched behind one ear, breaking our gaze. "Haven't quite figured that out yet. But, hey, two heads put together are bound to come up with something, aren't we?"

"Right." He said it with such lack of conviction it would have been better if he'd kept his mouth shut.

I added, "Well, it beats curling up in this hole and dying, right?"

"You bet." With a lot more confidence.

Grinning, I got to my feet and offered him a hand up. "Great. Here, let me show you around."

There's one thing about the Pit that's worse than the filth and the ugliness and the constant terror: the boredom. Doesn't help, of course, that boredom gives the terror good soil to put down roots, but to be honest, we could be awaiting our turns in the Palaces of Heaven and it still wouldn't be much better. Sometimes I felt so bored it hurt to think.

Showing Rathin around gave me something to do, but it didn't relieve the monotony as much as I'd hoped, since I was, after all, showing him around the same boring Pit I'd memorized weeks ago. It was a vast well, four hundred steps across, the Astet Above knew how deep. The floor was gray stone worn smooth by pacing feet, the walls were rough-hewn gray stone, but not rough enough to climb up. Lying on the floor and sitting against the walls were hundreds of rag-clad, filthy, miserable, and bored men, women, and some children.

The tour's highlight was introducing Rathin to the white fungus that made up our diet.

"Tastes like pork," I said, passing some to him.

He chewed, swallowed. I saw him restraining a gag. At last, in an affronted tone, he said, "Do you think we'll get very far in our partnership if we lie to one another?"

"I forgot to specify rotten pork. Sorry."

I heard once that human flesh tastes like pork, and because of that I sometimes suspected...well, the obvious. I didn't share that with Rathin. After I ate my fill of the rotten-flesh fungus, we rinsed our mouths out at the Pit's single spring. The water was metallic, almost sweet but not as thirst-quenching as it should be.

"And that," I said, drying my hands on tattered trouser legs, "completes our tour of the Pit."

"Lovely place," Rathin said. "When can we leave?"

"Soon as we figure out how."

He craned his head back, looking up at the walls. "Has anybody tried climbing—?"

"Yeah. It usually ends with a splat." I slapped my hand against my damp pant leg. The resulting sound illustrated far too clearly.

Rathin winced. "Right." Then, after a moment's further thinking, "Maybe Anweth can help."

"Your wizard friend? Does he know we're down here?"

"I suppose not. We got separated after an encounter with some bandits on the plains. And when I went looking for him...Well, it's unlikely he'll show up here. Unless he got captured, too."

"Not really something to hope for."

"I suppose not," he said again. He rested his chin on his knees, and his eyes took on a brightness I didn't like. "Too bad, though. Anweth could—"

"Watch it," I said.

"What?"

"Don't...get emotional about things. No matter how much you like your friend, don't smile when you think of him. And don't laugh no matter how funny something is. Never cry." Crying was no worse than the others, really, but it got on my nerves a lot more.

Rathin gave me an odd look, but after that there were no smiles, laughter, tears or distant looks from him. We discussed the possibility of overcoming the Pit-keepers with brute force, but it was an unlikely plan—they could easily match weakened, unarmed prisoners strength for strength. And then we were out of ideas. We fell silent, trying to think of more, but thinking, like most things in the Pit, soon lapsed into boredom, and I at least was done for the day.

That night, after a supper of fungus and a lot of water, Rathin and I lay down beside each other. There was some gossiping in the Pit, and I was sure somebody would think we were lovers, but good-looking as Rathin was, I felt filthy to the core, my clothes were so stiff with sweat they'd probably hurt to take off, and I was not in the mood at all. Rathin likely felt the same, because I could have been his sister for the way he treated me.

We did talk, though.

He asked me why he shouldn't show emotion in the Pit, and I explained my theory. I'd never shared it with anybody before, except Joslin—but that was back when I was new, and more willing to share things in general. No more. Sharing was too much like showing emotion, and I suspected the Pit-keepers quite literally ate that stuff up.

"So what do you think?" I asked when I had finished.

"If you're right, it's no wonder people don't last long down here. Every mother's child has to show how they feel sometimes—and Astet's Mercy, in a place like this, I imagine you must feel a lot."

Some people, facing death, do get emotional. But not most swordsellers. I was surprised at Rathin.

"Not me." I turned on my side. "But then, I'm no mother's child."

"You're not?" I wasn't certain if he was mocking me, or only asking to make conversation. But I answered.

"My mother...she was a swordseller. Ran off with every caravan that rolled through town, returned home for a fortnight or so to drink away her earnings, then ran away again soon as she could. Dad would've left, I think, if she hadn't stayed home long enough when they first married to whelp a few kids. Me, my sister, and my brothers." I stretched. "She named the oldest Corim—after the first caravan boss who'd hired her. Dad named the rest. I've always suspected that Corim was Corim's father..." I bit my tongue. It was ugly stuff I was saying, probably true but not kind to Corim, who had for a time been my favorite brother—and anyway, I was speaking angrily. "Anyway," I finished, "I might as well not have had a mother. Dad raised us fine, but she...better if she never existed."

"How's that?" I heard the rest of his question—Really? It would be better if she never existed, never birthed you? If you never existed? Luckily, Rathin seemed to sense I wasn't in the mood for conversation, because then he said, "Funny. I never thought of what it must be like to have a swordseller parent. I wondered, sometimes, about having children...probably best I don't."

"Maybe not," I said. "You're more thoughtful than my mother was, for sure. If you found the right girl and settled down with her..."

He made a strangled sound. "That is..."

"Don't mind me," I said. "I get like that sometimes. Supposing things."

"I'm not really the kind to settle down with a girl," he said, and we left it at that.

We slept, all of us in the Pit, and in the morning there were three fewer bodies on the cold stone floor. Rathin and I were still there, and I didn't let anything else matter.

It was Rathin's idea to ask the others to join us.

When it came to brains, two dozen were better than two, and when it came to brawn, four dozen arms were loads better than four. It was a sound idea. I couldn't say why I hated it so much.

"I just don't like working with so many people," I tried explaining to Rathin. "Too many different ways to go wrong. Or maybe it's because..."

"Yes?"

"If we get everybody in on this, we'll have to get everybody out."

"Of course."

"That could be pretty difficult."

He looked at me. Just looked. Some looks say everything that needs to be said and more.

We started by working our way around the Pit, stopping by each huddled body and murmuring that we'd like a few words at the spring.

Not all of them came. I hadn't expected them too, knowing how exhaustion and despair set in after you'd been down there a while, how you didn't feel like doing anything and then pretty soon you couldn't. About a dozen did show up, and that was great, through Rathin and I both knew without saying that we'd have to get the others out as well.

"What do you want to talk about?" The speaker was a woman in a sturdy traveling dress and fraying but stubbornly-holding-together braids. No swordswoman, but obviously practical; I liked her on sight.

"Let's talk about busting our way out of here," I said.

A graying-haired wisp of a man chuckled hoarsely. "Every mother's child of us will agree to that."

Rathin glanced at me, and I imagine I looked like I had a mouthful of manure with lemon garnish, because he said, "Even some of us who aren't mothers' children." Some laughed, probably thinking he had made a joke they just didn't get.

I shrugged. "Everyone wants to get out of here, whatever cliché you want to use to express it." The gray-haired man looked a bit miffed at that, but the others were listening eagerly. "Thing is, we don't have many options. There's no way all of us can climb those walls. Our best bet might be facing the Pit-keepers."

Our audience squirmed.

"Unless anyone has a better idea," I added.

If anyone did, she kept it to herself.

"I think," the practically-dressed woman said, "fighting the Pit-keepers would be the most direct way to save ourselves."

"We are unarmed," Rathin said, though not like he was disagreeing. "Fighting back will be dangerous."

"It's more dangerous and less noble to wait down here like bread stacked in a larder," she said.

Everyone, even Rathin, nodded agreement with her.

"Okay," I said, "here's the tricky part." They leaned closer—I was speaking quietly, though Astet only knew if the Pit-keepers listened in on us. If they did, our gathering by the spring already looked suspicious, but I couldn't help that. "I think that, whatever way the Pit-keepers come down to, er, feed, will also be the way for us to get up. But every time a Pit-keeper comes...we're asleep."

"And it's all but impossible to stay awake," a man said. Others nodded. "I've tried, but always..."

"Yeah," I said. "I think we've all tried. But we all do it alone. What if we helped each other? I think we should partner up tonight, and partners should do anything they can to keep each other awake—talking, singing, hitting..." A few chuckles at that.

"And then what?" someone back in the crowd asked. "Do we attack them tonight?"

"Maybe we should wait," the practical woman said. "After all, we don't know much about them. If we observed..." She didn't look happy about it—of course not; the Pit-keepers only came down for one reason, and if we did nothing tonight, someone was going to die. Probably more than one.

But if we attacked too soon, we all would. Every mother's child of us.

"Tonight," Rathin said, "if I give you the signal, we attack. If not...we wait."

"That's a good idea," the woman said. Others agreed. I met Rathin's eyes, and he nodded. He knew what he was doing, taking responsibility for whatever happened that night.

"Thank you," I said.

"What's the signal?" the woman intruded with her practicality.

Rathin pursed his lips, thinking. "Anybody here named Anweth?"

Nobody was.

"So if I call that name, you'll all know that's the signal for attack?"

Everyone nodded.

"Is there anything else that needs to be decided?" I asked, somewhat impatiently. Partly I was nervous that the Pit-keepers might be watching. Partly I was just through with people for the day. And maybe I was ashamed that I hadn't wanted to help save them because it was too difficult.

"One thing worries me." A thin, pale man with a narrow face said. By the tone of his voice I knew there would be trouble.

"Yes?"

"What if the reason we're all asleep when the Pit-keepers come has nothing to do with discipline or our failing at it? What if we're under a spell or something?"

A nervous buzz began among the group.

"Can the Pit-keepers work magic?"

Rathin shrugged. "Who knows?" Watching him, I knew he wished from the depths of his soul that his wizard friend Anweth was here. Though I had never met the man, I was wishing it myself.

"Let's assume they can't," I said. "If tomorrow we realize none of us managed to stay awake...we'll plan something else."

For a moment I thought the sallow young man would say more, but he didn't. His point was well-made, even I had to admit, but I was glad everyone accepted my suggestion, or at least didn't argue with it. For now, we had no better ideas.

Rathin and I partnered up that night. At first keeping awake was easy. We did what we had the night before—we talked.

"Why did you become a swordswoman?" he asked.

"Why did you become a swordsman? Why did your wizard friend become a wizard? Why does a tailor become a tailor, or an innkeeper an innkeeper?" Though in retrospect those last were bad suggestions. Skilled trades usually went to the eldest children. "I was the youngest in my family," I said, "as no doubt you were in yours. We pretty much do what we want."

"But why did you want it?" he asked. "I was thinking, I mean, about how your mother..."

"Yeah, that." I rolled to face the sky overhead, if there was indeed a sky up there. "The thing is, she always ran off with a smile on her face. She made it look like fun."

"Is it?"

With a gesture, I encompassed the Pit. "Pretty cruddy right now, actually."

He laughed. "And what about before?"

"It was...satisfying. I don't know how my mother felt, doing her work, but when I bring a caravan home safely, it feels good. Useful. I can't imagine her ever feeling that way—she seemed to love being irresponsible. But out there, driving off an attack, or watching for landslide or flood, protecting...it's not fun, not exactly, but I like it."

"Yes," he said. "Useful. That's it. Anweth once told me if I ever wanted to settle down, he could support us—it's probably true, wizards can be well paid. But I didn't want to settle. Living off somebody else, even somebody I...well, I'd feel useless."

"How do you think Anweth feels, following you everywhere?" I asked. I tried to imagine it myself, and couldn't—I'd never had any friends I cared enough to travel alongside for any length of time.

"He doesn't always follow." I heard a smile in Rathin's voice. "More often he drags me into things. He'll have his way one day, when I'm worn out swordselling and don't care so much about being useful..."

"Maybe I'll settle down one day, too," I said, testing the idea. "I don't want to have kids while I'm still on the road—I'm not sure I could find a man who'd put up with it, anyway. My father was unique."

"Find a man who'll travel alongside you."

"The road's no place to raise kids." But was a village you visited once, twice a year any better? I thought about it...about the road. I liked it. "What about you, Rathin? Ever considered having a family?"

"Not really..."

"What about Anweth? You could be an uncle to his children, or something like that."

"...It's a little complicated," he said.

"You just need to find a woman and go ahead from there."

"Pavadan..." He sounded strangled. "Are you trying to...propose something to me?"

"Not exactly." My tone was too casual, and I knew it gave me away.

Although we were supposed to keep talking, we couldn't find much to say after that.

My first hint that I had fallen asleep came when I was shaken awake.

"Pavadan," a voice whispered in my ear.

I sat up. "Rathin?"

"Come with me." His hand took my own. He sounded as if he were smiling.

"Did you see something? Look, I'm sorry I fell asleep..."

"It's all right. I think a lot of the others did, too, Pavadan—" His voice dropped even lower. "Be very quiet. I think they're in here right now."

"The Pit-keepers?"

"Yes. But look across the Pit—they left their door open."

I looked across a stretch of darkness. There—for a moment I thought I'd imagined it, but no, there really was a darker patch against the inky expanse of the walls.

"Let's go," Rathin said.

What about the others? I almost asked. I should have. But I didn't—with escape so close I could taste it, with the Pit-keepers wandering the night around us and only one way out, I didn't have the courage. It seemed Rathin didn't,

either. But come morning, we'd be free. I rose and ran with him across the Pit.

Each moment I expected to be stopped by a Pit-keeper's claws, but we made it, to a hole that had opened into the seamless rock. We slipped inside into a narrow tunnel lined with oily-burning torches. The smell was awful, rancid.

Rathin led me down the corridor, still holding my hand. Our steps rasped on the floor, too loudly. I hesitated to add to the noise, but I needed to ask:

"Do you think there's any chance of getting our weapons back? We should keep an eye out for an armory—"

"Good idea." He looked back and smiled. I'm no sentimentalist, but that smile made my heart flutter. We were really going to make it.

We began to pass more doors, mere gaps in the rock leading to stone-walled chambers. I peered in each, and stopped at one where torchlight glittered on steel.

"Rathin," I said, "here it is."

I grabbed the torch and slipped through the narrow gap, hardly noticing when my hand slipped from his. There were swords, spears, and battle axes, laid on tables and hanging on the walls around us. It didn't take me long to find mine—I'd recognize the red leather grip and that blade more nick than steel anywhere. I took it up, and behind me Rathin said, "Pavadan..."

There was naked longing in his voice. I turned, and instinct told me to keep a good grip on my sword; if it hadn't I would have dropped it from shock and then everything would be over.

The teeth changed first. Rathin's white, not-so-friendly smile grew, lengthened grotesquely, and the rest of his face and body changed with it. I saw the fingernails sprout into claws.

For a moment I thought it all had been a lie. That the real Rathin had never existed, that this was all some monstrous trick. But no. I knew Rathin had been real, that he had a friend named Anweth, that he was a younger child like myself, that like me he longed to be useful—and I knew two other things.

The real Rathin would never have left the others in the Pit, and I shouldn't have either.

And the Pit-keepers didn't take you for showing emotion, not just for that. In the Pit, you doomed yourself by caring for someone, by giving the 'keepers a form to borrow, one you trusted enough to follow to your death.

I hadn't survived the Pit because I was disciplined, I survived because I was cold, uncaring. Well, now I was warm and caring, and I planned to survive anyway.

I swung my sword. The Pit-keeper parried with its claws. Long ago I'd learned a little about two-handed fighting, and I still remembered some—my muscles did, at any rate—because as soon as my first blow was knocked aside, I made another with my hand holding the torch.

The Pit-keeper fell back, claws raised as if to shield it from the flame. My sword went under them, into something that seized at the blade like goo, and the thing went down. I pulled my weapon free, and with the torch still in my other hand I ran into the corridor and down it, back to the Pit.

As I ran, I shouted at the top of my lungs, "ANWETH!"

Maybe the Pit-keepers did put a sleeping spell on their prisoners. But I believe despair alone is wearying enough, and anyway, those being taken away never caused any commotion, because they were lead away by someone they loved. My screams woke every mother's child, and when I reached the Pit they were on their feet, ready to fight, or run, or anything else I suggested.

I waved my torch. "This way! Anybody who can use a weapon, listen up! I've found the armory!"

At the head of them came Rathin. I could have wept. After those first few moments, I'd believed with all my heart that he existed, but I hadn't be certain he wasn't led away in the night by something that looked like Anweth.

It was simple after that, though not

exactly easy or quick. We met no one and nothing on our way to the armory, and once we were armed—many of us also bearing torches—the Pit-keepers we did encounter weren't much trouble, though we did suffer injuries and even some losses from those long, slashing claws. There was a moment of white pain when I feared I'd lose my arm, but Rathin's blade ensured it was only my torch that went missing—down something's throat, most likely. It hardly mattered, because by that time we could see the light from the surface.

I paced before the entrance of the Pit-keeper's cave, dry prairie grass whipping at my trouser legs, picking at the bandage Maia, the practically-dressed woman, had made from strips of her skirt. I thanked her profusely, probably to excess.The night before I'd run out on her, on every mother's child in the Pit, and I didn't know how to make up for it.

My mother would have run out on them, too.

For a while we rested before the cave, in the hot sun and the cool breeze, waiting to think of something to do. Someone suggested collapsing the tunnel's entrance, and those who could set to that task enthusiastically, hammering with sword hilts and battleaxes until the rock gave in. If any

of the Pit-keepers survived, they'd have to find another way out.

With my injured arm, I could only watch. Three months I had been down there. I wasn't sure what to do with myself up here.

Rathin sat beside me. "Hey. I see you took up my battle cry for yourself." His smile faded when I didn't return it. "What's wrong?"

"When the Pit-keeper came for me, it came in disguise. It came as someone it knew I would follow...As you."

"Oh." He said a lot with that almost-word. His arm went around me. I thought I might start crying, but I didn't. Three months of holding in your emotions forms a habit.

"Thank you," he said. "For turning back. You didn't have to, you know. Once you'd found out the danger, you were already free of the Pit. You could have run."

"I couldn't have," I said. "But...thanks. A lot."

"What now?" Maia asked. "Do we look for a road? Wait for somebody to come by?"

"We wait," Rathin said. "A friend is looking for me."

"How can you tell?"

"Have you ever been the focus of a finding spell?"

"No..."

"When you are," Rathin said dryly, "you can tell."

"Anweth?" I asked.

"Of course."

I smiled for him.

I had already realized how things stood, and when the figure we first saw that afternoon drew closer and closer until it resolved into a slender, dark-robed young man with a silver wizard's circlet in his white-blond hair, I wasn't at all surprised when Rathin greeted him with a lover's kiss. Others might have been, but if they were troubled they didn't show it; these men were, after all, saving our lives.

Knowing why it couldn't have been made things easier. I was disappointed, but watching them speak, catching up on the events of the past few days—more romantic than it sounds—watching Rathin being so happy made things hurt less. Anyway, I was alive. I had a lot to be thankful for.

Anweth led us to a small plains town a few days' travel north. The townsfolk were as startled as you might imagine, but they let us stay in their temple of Astet, and brought blankets and hot soup. The next day, and every few days after, people began to head east and west along the long road, some carrying messages for others. In time, more messengers arrived, ready to escort the weak or timid home to their waiting families. Except me. I stayed in town and waited for a reason to go on.

Rathin gave me one. "Anweth and I are going to the head of the Jewel Trail. Do you want to come with us?"

"Would you mind?"

"Of course not." He looked shocked at the very idea. And Anweth, across the hall, looked up and smiled at me with no trace of jealousy. Of course, he had nothing to be jealous of.

"I'll come," I said. "Thanks for inviting me."

There's not much left to tell. Life goes on. At the head of the Jewel Trail we hired on with different caravans, but that's all right. There aren't that many caravans in the world; we're bound to meet up again sometime. And if we don't, at least we parted friends.

Time in the Pit changed me. I still don't show how I feel much, and I don't sleep so well some nights. And when it comes to what I want, what I plan for...that's changed, too, but maybe for the better. I think of settling down sometimes. But more often I think of reaching out, finding someone, starting something. Something good that I won't abandon, even when the road calls me. If need be, I'll carry it with me. Anything to keep it.

I want to love and be loved. As, I imagine, does every mother's child.

The Dollhouse

by

Magen Toole

Herein a matter of perspective...

Aldus carried rooms inside himself, a dollhouse of seven floors guarded by his ribcage. The walls were built between his lungs, behind his heart and among his other organs with the smokestack coming up to sit at the base of his neck, giving off fine smoke rings that puffed out of his nose from time to time. A neighborhood of people lived there: tailors, doctors, teachers and bakers, making homes of the rooms Aldus kept. He was not quite sure how they had gotten there, unable to clearly remember a time before or after them. Aldus believed they had appeared there the morning he awoke to find splinters in his bed, tiny finishing nails between his teeth. In the bathroom he stood before the mirror and traced a fresh raised line from his neck to his navel, as though his ribs had been pushed open, stretched out and pulled shut again, but bulging beneath the skin. Like Aldus's recollections, in time that too faded.

For many months Aldus woke as the occupants of the dollhouse slept and whenever he slept they woke, rising from their beds to begin their days. Booted feet stomped up and down staircases, babies cried and doors slammed, rattling mirrors on walls. Little voices traveled up Aldus's spine to color his dreams with their troubles and conversations, filling his head with the trivial strife of lives Aldus could not reach. At night he scratched across the thin topography of his chest, playing at his ribs like piano keys to deter them, but without avail.

"Stop it," he would groan into his pillow, tossing restlessly back and forth across his bed. "Stop it, stop it, I have to sleep. I have to work in the morning, don't you understand?"

The tiny occupants did not listen, or if they had they did not care. Each night Aldus could only half-sleep, waking to the sounds of couples fighting and children fussing and old men wringing their leathery hands. Each day he went to work at the office and felt tired, rubbing the sleep from his eyes and yawning wide into phones and during meetings. In the evenings he went home to eat dinner and crawl in bed knowing he would not rest, and soon began to dread it. Inside of him, the occupants went about their noisy lives unaffected by these difficulties, too consumed by their own to pay Aldus any mind.

After so long without reprieve, Aldus

would wake in a daze to the final sounds of shuffling feet and rustling blankets as the neighborhood slipped at last into sleep. He began letting his fingers run determinedly under the row of buttons of his pajama top, imagining stitches there. A bisecting zipper where his ribs met that he could undo and open up, looking inside his chest at the dollhouse, to squeeze, perhaps shake the people inside for keeping him up at night. It was then that Aldus knew the dollhouse was driving him mad, the occupants sighing and moaning in his sleep about the dreary minutiae of cheating spouses, sick children and mortgages past due. He knew he must do something, or risk letting his sanity steal away in an unending parade of boot-heels and voices.

At his wit's end, one morning Aldus took a knife from the kitchen drawer, prepared to silence the people inside him. In the bathroom mirror he traced the raised line from his collarbone to his belly with the blade, splitting himself down the middle. He took the walls made of his ribs in hand and worked them gently apart until the bones and plaster gave way. They were divided by a seam and hinges and he pulled the dollhouse open wide, searching the floors and rooms where its tenants slept. There were nearly one hundred of them now, generations of parents and children, grandmothers, grandfathers

"Stop it," he would groan into his pillow, tossing restlessly back and forth across his bed. "Stop it, stop it, I have to sleep. I have to work in the morning, don't you understand?"

and old floppy dogs. They were tucked away safely in their beds all but for one. A little boy of five, or maybe six, sat at his bedside in tired pajamas, his sheets and blankets looking equally worn-through, his eyes and hands clasped tight in prayer.

"Dear Lord," the boy murmured, his clumsy whispers made louder by the silence, "please bless us, my Mother and Father and Robert and me. Please fix the leaks in our roof so that our beds stay dry, so that Robert won't be so sick all the time and Father doesn't stay up late worrying and Mother doesn't cry. Lord, please bless us and keep us safe."

Hearing this, Aldus's anger dissolved. Even for his strife he could not harm a child so small, especially one as quiet and reverent, and dressed so plainly in second-hand clothes. He abandoned the knife on the bathroom counter and took

23

up the cotton balls from the cabinet instead, using them to plug the holes in the child's roof and packing them in tight.

As the boy crawled into his bed to sleep Aldus closed his chest again, sewing it up with needle and thread. That night after dinner he lay down to sleep and heard boots stomping and doors slamming, old dogs barking the same as before. Through the din, rather than sighs and complaints he found tiny voices hushed in prayer instead, asking the Lord for patience and gentleness. Babies still cried and mirrors still rattled on the walls, but plugging his ears with the cotton from the cabinet, Aldus slept nonetheless.

Red Truck

by
William C. Rasmussen

Herein the mundane and the monstrous

The red truck was there again, I noticed.

My wife and I---both of us sixty, retired, and with time to kill---had seen it a half-dozen times or more over the past couple weeks: a late-model, red, Dodge Ram 1500 Crew Cab pickup truck, perched idling at the exit gate of a nearby subdivision and possibly watching over the construction underway across the street like a brooding sentinel.

This clear spring morning, as Carol and I drove north on Houston Levee Road in Shelby County, TN, my curiosity got the better of me. As we neared the Ram, I flipped my left turn indicator on, swung across the street, and pulled up alongside the truck. I pushed the power window button, waited for my window to descend, then, smiling, motioned to the driver to roll down his window as well. He simply ignored me and nothing happened.

I waited a moment, listening to his engine rumble like a hungry beast, and tried to see through the truck's darkly-tinted windows. A vague feeling of unease swept over me then, raising the fine hairs at the back of my neck.

"Hon," Carol said, lightly touching my thigh, "why don't we leave now?"

"Yeah, okay." I patted her hand, still distracted by the unknown male driver. And that's all I was able to determine due to the truck's unusually dark camouflage: that there was a man behind the wheel, not a woman. And while I stared at the truck, I glimpsed a strange symbol on its front quarter panel. It appeared to be about a foot-high caricature or cartoon drawing of

I checked the rear-view mirror this time for any sign of the truck following us, but came up empty. I let out a small sigh of relief. Why am I being so paranoid? I wondered. The guy just didn't feel like chatting...

some sort, depicting a darkly-garbed man with a black hat and black mask covering his eyes, holding something in his hands. I couldn't make out anything further about the design, however, as I quietly backed our Honda CR-V out of the driveway, and once again entered traffic heading north.

"Jay, what was that all about?" Carol asked after we had put some distance between us and the strange vehicle.

"You got me. I was just trying to be friendly. You know—tease the driver about what he was doing there. Geez!"

"How do you know it was a 'he'?"

I stole a peek at my wife before returning my attention to the road. "Well, about all I could see was the outline of a guy." I glanced at her again. "Beyond that I couldn't say."

"Why'd he ignore us?"

"Beats me," I said.

I checked the rear-view mirror this time for any sign of the truck following us, but came up empty. I let out a small sigh of relief. *Why am I being so paranoid? I wondered. The guy just didn't feel like chatting...*

Brushing aside these troubling thoughts, I glanced again at Carol and said, "Did you see the design he had on his truck?"

"No, what design?"

"Ahh...it was nothing. I'm not even sure what I saw."

Out of the corner of my eye I saw Carol look at me quizzically. I'm not sure why I decided not to tell her what I'd glimpsed, only that for some reason the drawing had struck me as a little peculiar. But, once again, I swept the feeling of unease from my mind as easily as brushing crumbs off the dinner table.

We went about our business the rest of the day, and on our return home that afternoon, I was secretly happy to see that, as we passed by its regular spot, the red truck was gone.

The next few days passed without any truck sighting, and the inner turmoil that I had felt during and following my lone confrontation with the faceless driver waned until it seemed like nothing more than a distant memory.

Until the afternoon I spotted a red truck in line about four or five cars behind us as Carol and I drove to the grocery store.

"Shit."

"What's wrong?" Carol said.

"I think the red truck might be following us."

"What?!" she squealed, twisting around in her seat to look out the back window.

"I can't tell for sure," I said, still

peeking at the rear-view mirror, "but there's a red truck behind us, a few cars back, and it might be a Dodge Ram."

"You think it's the same truck?"

"I don't know. Let's see if it follows us into the store's parking lot."

I hung a left at the next stoplight and made my way down to the Kroger Store, pulling into the huge parking lot. After swinging into a stall a bit removed from the cluster of cars already parked nearby, I turned my attention back to the red truck, which was waiting on traffic in the left-turn lane at the stoplight. It finally made the turn, chasing another car through the yellow light, and cruised down the street I had just traveled, continuing on past the grocery store.

Unconsciously, I let out a sigh of relief. I dropped the can of pepper spray I had latched onto into the small compartment between our front seats. My hands felt hot and sweaty.

"Whew," Carol said. "Do you think it was--?"

"I don't know," I snapped. "It wasn't tailing us, it probably wasn't even the same truck."

"Okay..." she said, put off by my tone.

"Come on," I said a little softer, killing the engine. "Let's get our shopping done."

I slid out of the SUV and Carol did likewise.

I spotted a red truck several times over the next few weeks while driving around, with and without my wife. I had no idea if it was our truck, but the frequency of its appearance behind me in traffic ruled out, in my opinion, any chance of it being totally coincidental. I never mentioned it to Carol, either, for vanity, I guess. Having spent most of my life in the criminal investigative arena, solving cases for the county and later assisting attorneys in similar fashion, I was annoyed to discover that despite my highly decorated past, I was currently at a loss to expose the mystery behind the driver of the red truck. On a couple of occasions I had even tried to double back behind him to ascertain his license plate. But each effort had proven fruitless as the Dodge Ram easily slipped off in another direction, disappearing like a wraith. Even my many law enforcement contacts were of no help; they calmly explained to me that I was probably being a bit paranoid, but even if something indeed was up, without a license plate their hands were tied. They said to be careful. Well, I had said to myself, I thought I was being careful.

Then, one night around 10:00 or so, I was in the living room catching the late news when I heard a low rumbling sound coming from the street outside. Carol was surfing the Net on the computer in our bedroom and couldn't hear it. It sounded like a dog growling, but I had a funny feeling it was actually our red truck, the driver nudging the gas pedal to catch our attention.

I pried apart the blinds of our front window and peeked out. Sure enough, the red Dodge Ram was out there, idling at the curb on the far side of our narrow street. I wasn't certain what I should do. Confront him and run the risk of danger? Or simply wait him out and see what happens? But before I could come to a decision, he gunned the engine one last time and pulled away from the curb.

I raced to the front door and threw it open, hoping to catch his tag as he sped away. I was too late. But not too late to pick out on his driver's-side, front quarter panel, as he made a left turn a short distance away, the odd, cartoon-like design I had first glimpsed almost a month ago. It seemed to glow in the dark, like it had a life of its own. Strange, I thought. But it was him, definitely him.

What do you want? I wondered.

A while later, after I had resettled into my La-Z-Boy and Carol had come up for air from her Internet surfing, I told her what happened. She wasn't happy that I hadn't called her.

"I've tried to cash in favors with some of my buddies at the Sheriff's Office, to try and ID this guy, but that hasn't panned out yet. And now this...weirdo...knows where we live!"

"Oh, God, hon!" she said. "Are we in trouble? Is he dangerous?"

"I'm not sure... We *do* need to be careful from now on," I said, embracing her. "At least until I find some way to put an end to this madness."

"Jay, I'm scared," she said, squeezing me tightly.

"We'll be fine," I said with false bravado. "Just let me handle it."

I didn't have any game-changing plan or strategy that I was prepared to implement, and it bothered me. All I was doing now was reacting to the machinations of the red truck's operator instead of doing something proactive. It frustrated the hell out of me. Even more than usual, because this time Carol was involved, too.

I had already called on the resident manager at the small apartment complex where the unknown driver chose to idle his truck, and had also gone across the street to chat with the foreman of the ongoing construction project. Neither person had any information I could use in my efforts to identify our stalker; in fact, the female resident manager and the burly foreman swore they had never even seen the red Dodge Ram in question!?

With such horrendous results under my belt, I was certain I was going to lose my mind before too long. The only saving grace appeared to be the fact that neither Carol nor I had observed our truck for several days, not since the night the faceless driver had surprised me with his unexpected visit. *Perhaps he's given up*, I thought hopefully. *Maybe... But given up what?*

All we could do now, I guessed, as PO'd as it made me, was maintain our vigilance: be careful outside around the house, and use special caution when we drove around the city and suburbs while running our usual errands.

But Carol and I slowly relaxed our guard after a couple more uneventful days passed by. Until one night she complained that her acid reflux would not go away with her usual medicine.

"Do you need me to get something stronger?" I said.

"Yeah, I guess I could try the Extra-Strength Prevacid."

"Let me run up to Walgreens," I said. "Will you be okay for a few minutes?"

"Yes. Just hurry back."

I gave her a quick kiss, then dashed out to the garage and started up our SUV. It was around 11:30, and I was fairly sure the pharmacy stayed open until midnight. I backed out and closed the garage door before speeding off on my errand of mercy. The prospect of running into our M.I.A. red truck at this late hour was as remote as the possibility of me being struck by lightning during my short trip.

I was barely gone twenty minutes.

But even as I crept down our narrow, dimly-lit street, I knew something was wrong. I could sense it somehow; my thinning head of hair stood up for a second and my back tingled as if I'd been in close proximity to that improbable lightning strike.

Sitting innocently at the curb in front of our house was a red Dodge Ram. *Our truck.*

"Shit," I whispered in disbelief.

A welter of emotions overwhelmed me: anger, fear, and worry topping the list. Adrenaline flooded my system; the fight or flight syndrome kicked in. Face hot and flushed, I stomped on the gas pedal as my line-of-sight narrowed in tunnel vision. I stood on the brake seconds later, trying not to burn rubber as I skidded to a halt abreast of the truck.

Squinting through the passenger window, I spotted the odd, cartoon-like design on the side panel and attempted to see if our inscrutable driver was behind the wheel. But with the poor street lighting, the late hour, and his heavily-tinted windows, it was difficult to determine. I was fairly certain that he had already exited, though.

I gunned our SUV around the Dodge Ram, catching more of the design's details in my peripheral vision, and swung into our driveway, choosing not to raise the garage door and risk alerting him to my presence. Killing the engine, I slid out of the car and quietly closed the door. I moved cautiously around the garage toward our front entrance before realizing that not only had I failed to get a good look at his license plate in my earlier haste, I had also left the canister of pepper spray in the SUV.

"Shit!" I mumbled for the second time in less than a minute.

With sweat dripping from my forehead, I knew that time was of the essence. I decided to take my chances, and continued on toward the front door, whose familiar, softly-glowing porch light belied the underlying tension I was feeling right now.

I paused momentarily at our solid oak door, unsure of whether I should enter quietly or barge in and make my presence known. This guy had gotten into my head a little more than four weeks ago, and now he had gotten into my house---I decided I'd had quite enough of him. Right or wrong, I twisted the door knob, which was unlocked, and charged in calling out to my wife.

"Carol! Carol, where are you!?"

I moved deliberately through our living room, scanning the area for the intruder and latching onto the fat Maglite I kept by my recliner in case of a power outage.

"Carol!" I shouted again, a second or two before she poked her head out of the kitchen at the rear of our house, a grim look etched upon her face.

"Jay, look out!" she cried.

Her warning pulled me up short but, before I could react, a large figure hiding in the hallway fell upon me, striking me hard on the back of the head with a heavy, blunt object. As I fell to the floor, the flashlight slipping out of my grasp, a subtle smell, not unlike rotten eggs, trickled up my nose. Then I passed out.

"...Jay...Jay...! Wake up, please!"

I slowly came to on the living room floor with Carol hovering over me, her hands alternately caressing and shaking my face.

"Wha—what happened?" I said, trying to sit up as a bout of vertigo washed over me. I gently touched the back of my head, where a golf ball-sized knot trickling blood throbbed in time with my heartbeat. "Geez," I moaned as a sour taste filled my throat. "Are *you* okay, hon? Is he gone?" I struggled to stand, my eyes searching the room for the truck driver, finding the front door slightly ajar.

"He's gone, Jay, sit back down. I'm fine, too."

I fell more than sat down on our couch, my jumbled mind trying to piece together the puzzle of what had happened.

"What time is it?" I asked, elbows on my knees, hands cradling my head.

"It's a little after midnight. You've been unconscious for a couple minutes. We need to get you to the hospital."

"I'll be okay," I said, the bitter taste in my mouth receding. "How'd he get in?"

"He knocked on the front door right after you left. I thought you'd forgotten something, and opened it without checking. He came right on in and...the next thing I remember, you were barging into the house. Then he hit you with a pipe or tire iron, I guess. Oh, Jay, you might have a concussion. We have to get you to the Emergency Room!"

"No," I said, reaching for the phone. "I need to call the police first, have them come out here and look around, take our statements. Then we'll see..." I rubbed my head again with my free hand, blood streaking my fingers. "Hon, grab a towel for me, please. I'm still bleeding." Then I carefully punched in the number for the Shelby County Sheriff's Office.

Ten minutes later a pair of sheriff's deputies knocked on our front door, followed shortly by Dave, a former co-worker and friend of mine, who made the scene out of personal concern as well as professional courtesy. My buddy was already aware of the ongoing trouble we had been having with the enigmatic truck driver, but Carol and I repeated the events of the past month in chronological order anyway, culminating with the home invasion and assault at our house. Meanwhile, the two deputies scoured the house's interior and the front yard for any pertinent evidence or clues, but found none. And due to the fact that I had again been unable to ID the intruder's license plate and had shortly thereafter been knocked out cold, the only valuable information I provided for Dave and his incident report was the description of the Dodge Ram and its odd, cartoon-like design. Surprisingly, although Carol had supposedly been alert and relatively untouched throughout the ordeal, her memory of the nightmarish ten minutes or so alone with the intruder was sketchy at best. I believed strongly that the stress and trauma of the incident had given her temporary amnesia, and hoped that time would eventually lift the gauzy veil that now enshrouded a portion of her mind like a dense fog.

As soon as Dave and the deputies departed, Carol convinced me to let her drive us to the hospital: obviously, I might have suffered a concussion from the blow to the head, not to mention the fact that I probably needed a couple of stitches; in Carol's case, I simply wanted to ensure that she was physically all right, and a thorough examination would help ease my mind, as well as hers.

In due time I received four stitches and a diagnosis of a mild concussion; Carol received a clean bill of health, physically anyway; and we both received an ironic shock on discovering our late-night incident's catalyst which I'd forgotten on the floor of our SUV's front passenger seat---the pharmacy package containing Carol's medicine.

Three hours later we were back home.

We spent the next several days holed up in our house like a couple of hermits. My head still throbbed sporadically and I was prone to bouts of dizziness and nausea, but my health was improving steadily. Carol appeared to be none the worse for wear, although at times she exhibited sudden, unlikely episodes of moodiness and silence; but I was more concerned about her bruised mental state and how the ordeal would affect her in the long run. She still had not come to terms with the events of that night or her selective amnesia, the answer to either of which would shed light on what actually happened to her and what the intruder wanted. I was fairly certain that sexual assault had not occurred, but then it begged the question: what *did* happen?

A week after the incident we began venturing outside, taking short trips in our SUV with Carol behind the wheel. And each time we passed the spot where our red truck used to sit, we exhaled a collective sigh of relief at its extended absence. Sure, we wanted the driver to be caught and brought to justice, but at the same time, we were just as pleased inside to discover that he had most likely gone into hiding as a result of what he'd done to us. Dave had come by a few days earlier to check on us and advise that no leads had surfaced in the investigation. So, I had already begun to believe that the case would likely end up as a dead file.

Another day or two passed before I noticed that, even as my condition improved, Carol's worsened. She was losing a lot of sleep and appeared fatigued all the time now; she was also losing weight and the pounds sliding off her left her already thin face and frame even more lined and slack than ever;

and her periods of moodiness and quiet had become more frequent. I suggested a visit to her physician and she agreed. But after a battery of tests, her doctor found nothing physically wrong with her, suggesting only that she increase her intake of "B" vitamins, eat regularly, rest often and try to get more sleep, which he hoped to solve by slipping her a prescription for mild sleeping pills.

"How're you feeling?" I asked her from the shotgun seat on the drive home.

"All right, I guess... I just feel so tired and sluggish lately."

I paid special attention to her response, stared at her once-beautiful face, which now seemed almost as rough and dried out as a lifelong sun-worshiper. She looked to me like she was shriveling up right before my eyes. *What the hell is wrong with you, Carol?*

"Do you remember anything more about that night, hon, anything at all?"

She glanced at me quickly, tearing her eyes from the road for just a second. "I've been thinking about it a lot lately..." she replied. "And one thing I do recall is him...putting his hand on top of my head...and placing his other hand...in the center of my chest..." She paused, her face frowning in concentration. She started to cry then, softly.

"What's wrong, baby? What did he do?" I thought my worst fears had been realized.

"No, Jay, it isn't what you're thinking." She sniffled, peeked at me again. "He mumbled something I couldn't make out, like he was praying or chanting. Then, after several seconds, he pulled his hands off me and backed away. That's...that's all he did."

"It's a start," I said, stroking her upper leg, my mind swirling with ideas.

"But the weird thing," she continued, "is that when he removed his hands, it felt like he took something from me. That something was missing after that. I can't explain it..."

"All right, hon," I said, shaking my head over the possible ramifications of her story. "Let's not worry about it right now. Just get us home. We'll talk about it later."

We talked about it later, and often over the next few days. I had no answers for her, but I had a couple of theories—none of them good. I couldn't quite wrap my head around the seemingly innocuous actions of our intruder; but the more I thought about it, the more I realized that he *had* done something to Carol that night, something bad. And when her physical condition deteriorated drastically soon thereafter, and a return trip to her doctor offered no explanation, I knew one thing, and one thing only—Carol's life depended entirely on me finding our mysterious truck driver and coercing him to remove whatever pox or plague he had loosed upon her during his late-night visit.

A week has passed and the two of us, in our SUV, now cruise the surrounding streets from sunup to well past sunset, searching for the elusive red truck. I drive now, since Carol's motor functions have become impaired and she has extreme difficulty simply walking. Always a thin woman, she's now down to eighty-five pounds and her emaciated body looks like the desiccated husk of a butterfly cocoon. She can barely talk. Sometimes what she says makes no sense at all. She's dying. And I think I finally know why.

You see, the driver of the red truck didn't infect Carol by giving her something—he caused her to slowly shrivel and deteriorate by *taking* away something. Her essence, her vitality, her *soul*, if you will. Carol, herself, had stated that she felt like something was missing after he'd touched her that night. I finally pieced it all together when I remembered the details of the perplexing cartoon design on the truck fender. The night the proverbial "shit hit the fan," I got a good look at the drawing. It was definitely a darkly-garbed and *caped* man, wearing a dark brimmed hat with a black mask covering his eyes. But what I also saw was the large, stuffed brown bag he clasped in his hands, like a bandit. It seemed to be glowing, as if with life. The caricature-design was that of a thief, a robber, a stealer of *souls*.

I recalled as well the mild odor of rotten eggs I smelled as I fell to the living room floor the night he struck me. The scent of rotten eggs—sulfur---in legends has always been an indicator of the presence of Satan or his minions. As preposterous as it sounds, I now believe that our truck driver is an otherworldly emissary whose mission is to lure unsuspecting people into his trap and steal the essence of their lives, their souls. And the reason why no one else seems to remember the red truck sitting innocently at its post just off a main street, alert for victims? Apparently it's only visible to those he believes are sensitive or susceptible to him and his nefarious agenda.

Again, I may be completely off base with this, but I doubt it. In any case, it would be understatement to say that "time is of the essence." But it is. Because not only is my once-beautiful, loving Carol wasting away before my very eyes, but this morning, when I gazed into the bathroom mirror while shaving, I noticed the sudden onset of old age lines creasing my features and a conspicuous sagginess to my cheeks that hadn't been there the day before. I feel so tired now. I think after the truck driver slammed me to the floor he took something from me as well. Something that Carol didn't remember seeing him do, but which I also need to stay alive.

Despite the fact that the sun set hours ago, I continue to drive the dark streets with Carol beside me, hoping to locate the stealer of souls. I will continue as long as I am able.

God help me.

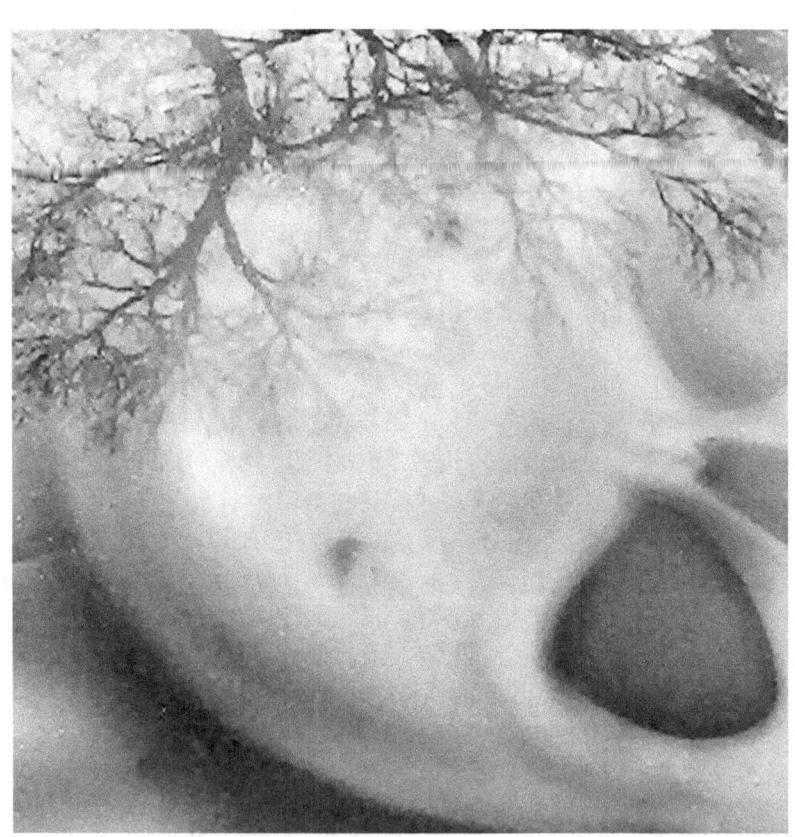

We Are Family

by
Simone Martel

Herein, definitions and utility and possibilities.

Bella rushed into the bedroom, struck a match, lit the incense in the brass, Isis-shaped holder, then fell back onto the bed, hands on her belly, her long white cotton skirt fanning out on the bedspread, her black braid an exclamation point on the pillow.

"My mother never loved me." she said to the ceiling. "What if I can't love my baby? Ever since I was a little girl playing with dolls I've wanted a baby, but now I'm scared. Freddy."

Freddy, leaning in the doorway, rubbed her hand over her crew cut.

"You're nuts."

Bella patted the bedspread and Freddy joined Bella, heaving her onto her large bosom and hugging both arms around Bella's shoulders.

"You love me, even if my mother doesn't," Bella said.

"'Calling Doctor Freud.'"

I don't believe she referred to me. I'm just a seven inch tall Freud Action Figure. A gag gift—nasty term— from Freddy to Bella, a comment on Bella's navel-gazing—another nasty term. From my place on the table on a dust-darkened circle of lace, I looked across at the bed, at Bella's pale bare feet and Freddy's in thick rag wool socks, the foreshortened lengths of their bodies, to the carved Mexican headboard to which Freddy sometimes tied Bella's wrists with soft, gauzy scarfs. I have a new home, now, one I prefer. I'm glad I no longer stand watch near the foot of their bed.

How did the real Freud feel about lesbians? I've no idea. My grasp on history is loose. (Though I know more than enough about the cult of Isis.) After all, I'm not a doctor, I'm an Action Figure, though back then I saw as little action as the purple vibrator to my right on the doily. It was two inches taller than I, but we shared a similar shape. However, the conceited brass Isis incense burner to my left was all curves; bulging breasts, belly and thighs. Isis considered herself a fertility figure and often chanted prayers to herself, but I don't recall if she was doing so on that particular day.

From her pillow, Bella broke the silence. "Are we just going to cuddle?"

"You don't want to shake it loose." Freddy sat up on the creaking bed. "Got to get back to work, anyhow. Don't brood about your mom. I'll bring home dinner."

42

"Sal's pizza?"

"You're not eating that crap."

"Bossy."

After Freddy left, the motorcycle roar fading, Bella sat up and padded out of the room. Moments later, I heard the back door slap shut.

"She forgot to blow you out," I complained to Isis. "She'll burn the house down and us in it."

"Stop your fussing, old man."

Later, Bella returned with a vase of roses she set on the table behind Isis, frowning at the trail of gray ash that lay over the doily.

"She might dust."

"Hush." Isis said. "I'm sensing a bad aura. Oh, dear!"

At that moment, Bella's hand went to her belly. Her face froze, then crumpled. "Not again!" She ran to the bathroom, sobbing. Isis began to sob, too.

I wanted to comment that she was a very poor fertility goddess.

When Bella and Freddy returned from the hospital, Bella went to bed in a flannel nightgown buttoned to her chin, her black hair lose.

"Will you let people know? Call my mom?"

"I'll take care of everything."

Freddy brought Bella a mug of tea, magazines, extra pillows, thumping around the room.

"I don't know if I can go though with it again," Bella said, over her tea.

"Sure you can, when you're stronger."

"What if I can't have a baby–ever? What if I'm being punished for resenting my mother for not loving me?"

"Don't talk so much. Rest."

I could've told you Bella wouldn't stay in bed, though. Soon she sat by the window or paced the narrow space between bed and closet. Once, standing listlessly, she held a pillow against her stomach and studied herself in the mirror with hope in her eyes and despair in the set of her mouth. Then she knelt before Isis to light yet another incense stick.

"Help me make a family."

Next morning, she woke first and lay, eyes open, beside Freddy. Twice, she touched Freddy's round shoulder, finally rousing her with a kiss on the cheek. Freddy's wide mouth stretched into a smile.

"S'up? You look better this morning."

"I am. I had a thought, maybe a dream." She raised herself on an elbow, her face close to Freddy's. "You could try."

"Me! But—you always wanted to have a baby."

"I want a family. Please consider it?"

Freddy closed her eyes. "Brenda wanted a family."

"That's so sad."

"After she got sick she said she regretted waiting. She really wanted a baby."

"And I really want one, too." Bella sat up in bed, pressing her palms together, beseeching.

"And I want to make you happy."

"I love you," Bella said. "We're so great together."

"When Brenda died, I thought I'd never find someone new to love."

"But you did. Me." Bella pressed her hands to her heart, her hair flowing over her shoulders.

"With that convertible-driving redhead. Finding someone to love has never been your problem, you little slut."

Bella giggled as Freddy reached up, grabbing her wrists roughly, crushing them together in one large hand. They made love, then, and Isis crooned with pleasure, while I wished to turn my bearded face to the wall, or at least close my plastic eyes.

I knew Freddy had done it when she began making extra trips to the bathroom at night.

"I have to pee constantly," she complained in the morning.

"That's normal, that's good."

"My boobs hurt."

"Freddy..." Bella pleaded with her. "You're an amazing person. Once you make up your mind to do something, you go out and do it. You're pregnant, now. You should be happy."

"It feels weird."

Bella's eyes went to the stack of well-used books on her nightstand. Freddy noticed.

"Yeah, yeah, I'll look at your books."

"Educate yourself," Bella said as Freddy left the room. "The one with the black and white photographs is beautiful..."

"Beautiful!" I began, but Isis hushed me.

Alone, Bella sat on the edge of the bed and pulled the book onto her lap, opening it to a marked page.

"There's no justice in the world," Isis said, sniffing. "She's taking it well, but her heart's breaking."

Bella didn't cry, though. In fact, she managed a smile as she looked up from the book, slammed the glossy pages shut, and strode out, her skirt swirling around her ankles.

Weeks passed. Calling it Indian Summer, Bella slipped on sun dresses in the morning and spent little time in the bedroom. With only Isis for company, the hours dragged. In the afternoons, hot sun burned through the westward facing window. One morning, as Freddy, on all fours, searched under the bed for a sock, the sound of Bella retching in the bathroom startled her so that she

44

hit her head on the frame. She stood, hand on bristly hair, as Bella came in, wiping her grinning mouth.

"You're knocked up."

"I'd say it was an accident, but..."

"An accident, yeah. You went to the clinic without me?"

"I knew it'd stick this time. And I was right. I never barfed the other times."

"Is that required?" I asked Isis. "Pity."

"But two babies at once?" Freddy's forehead wrinkled.

"I always wanted two. This way we'll get past the diapers faster."

Freddy sat on the bed, heavy, silent, pulling on the socks.

"You're thinking, 'Can we afford this?'" Bella asked.

Freddy shrugged.

"This is wonderful news," Isis said to me. "And all my doing. They'll be like twins."

"Don't be stupid," I said back. "Not even siblings."

"In the eyes of the Goddess they are."

"In eyes of the world, they are not."

In time, the babies were born. First, though, more sounds of barfing tormented me. As Bella and Freddy swelled, the bedroom walls drew in. Bella sat on the bed, examining her pale legs for spider veins, while Freddy glared at herself in the mirror.

"I look like a pregnant man. You're

"That bitch left me on my side," Harry Potter said, lying on the little round carpet at my feet.

lovely, though."

"Except my legs."

Then Freddy disappeared for a day and a half and returned with a bundle she called Noah, with a wrinkled red face under a yellow cap. She nursed him in bed, her huge breasts hanging out, splayed, and changed his diapers at a new changing table, taking a cloth diaper from the stack and dropping the soiled one into a diaper pail lined with a blue plastic bag.

"Christ, I have squat mustard under my nails."

Soon after, Bella brought home a red-faced bundle with a crest of black hair. She called it Nora.

The babies cried together and separately. Sometimes, to stop the clamor, Freddy clamped Nora to her breast; sometimes Bella nursed Noah, too exhausted to differentiate. No one slept more than an hour at a time.

"I feel stupid," Freddy said. "I want my brain back. I want my life back."

Those were grim times; fall, then winter.

"It's freezing out. The babies mustn't

get a chill." Bella yanked together the orange velvet curtains Freddy had drawn apart.

Two am and two pm were indistinguishable with the sun shut out, the bedside lamps burning and a portable heater pinging in the corner. In that overheated room, Freddy's upper lip gleamed with sweat. Dirty dishes piled up, and clothes, newspapers, and mail drifted over the bed and down the tumbled pillows to the carpet.

"I hate this mess. I miss my job. What's wrong now?"

Bella bent her head, her braid coiled on her shoulder. "I'm so happy here in our nest, except...you're ruining it."

Gradually, though, the mood in the room lightened. With spring on the horizon, Freddy spread the curtains and even cracked open the window, letting in gusts that rustled newspapers and blew dust bunnies over the floor. Tidying, at last, Bella unburied her flute and played a tune on it for Freddy and the babies. Later, Freddy, kneeling by the bed, performed a puppet show with socks, and the two babies lying in the crooks of Bella's arms, cracked what Bella called their first social smiles, rather than grimaces caused by gas.

Freddy returned to work; Bella cared for the two babies who had outgrown their bassinets and sat in identical carriers on the bed, flopped back, bellies foremost. For a time, they stared at their own hands, splayed like starfish in front of their noses. Later, though, they reached out and joined hands, tiny fingers entwined, and gazed at each other from their carriers. When Bella dressed them, she pulled clothes from a single wicker basket brimming with colorfully patterned t-shirts, pants, socks. When they grew old enough for toys, they played with rattles, mirrors, plush round balls and stacking cups from a single bin. Then Noah began to crawl and Nora screamed with rage, because she could not follow. That was a difficult time, though brief, I suspect, since Nora was determined to keep up with Noah. I can't say for sure when Nora learned to crawl, though, because shortly after Noah became mobile, Bella announced, "Time to baby-proof this place."

Kneeling at the low table, she swept the purple vibrator, Isis, the doily, the silver matchbox, and other knickknacks, including myself, into a cardboard box. The lid came down.

"Goddess help us," Isis said.

The boredom! We objects need a world to watch. Eventually, Isis stopped talking. My thoughts grew darker, then black, then null, until the box joggled, was dragged loudly over the floor, and opened. In the square of light, I saw Bella's face, eyes small and red, freckled nose wet. The box flipped over and I

46

crashed face-down, objects raining on my back. I heard Bella pull a suitcase from under the bed and throw something into it from the mess on the floor.

"Goodbye, old man!" Isis called to me. "Blessings upon you."

Dresser drawers scraped open, wire hangers jangled in the closet, then heavy footsteps—Freddy's boots—came close and stopped by the bed.

"I don't want a husband." Bella sneered the word. "I don't want to be a wife, saying 'we never talk,' stuck here, wondering what's going on out there, why you come home mad." She sounded breathless, as if she'd been talking a long time.

Then Freddy's deeper voice answered more slowly. "I'm stressed from work. You know the new boss sucks. I'll try not to—"

"–Shut down? Close me out? We're such clichés!" The suitcase clicked. "I'll pick up Nora from softball. We'll stay with my mom."

"Your mom?"

"Where else can I go? I have no money."

"I give you money."

Bella shouted incoherent syllables from the living room, then the front door banged. I heard Freddy lurching though the house, muttering, rattling keys, then the front door again.

Hours later, footsteps crossed the front porch. As the key turned in the lock, a high-pitched voiced asked, "Where's Nora?"

I couldn't make out Freddy's reply, lost the howls that followed.

Where did Freddy sleep that night? She never came into the bedroom. Perhaps she slept near the boy. In any case, the crying stopped and the darkness was silent. The next day, I heard Noah following Freddy through the house, whining, complaining, persuading in breathless paragraphs that reminded me so much of Bella I had to remind myself that the boy wasn't related to her at all. By evening, Freddy sounded worn out.

"I need you to play by yourself now while I make an important phone call."

The boy entered the bedroom, breathing loudly. Seeing the disorder on the floor, he picked me up and turned me around, close to his chubby face. He touched my beard. Then, clutching me like a trophy, he carried me across the hall into a room with a bunk bed, upper and lower bunks unmade, stuffed animals lolling on the blankets. When the boy turned, a doll house careened into view and grew larger as he lunged toward it, thrusting me into a room next to a mouse in a frilly blue dress and white apron. Noah knelt, staring in. Then he got up and retreated to the bottom bunk, scrunching back into the disordered blankets. Hunched over, he started thumbing something close to his face.

"They were such a happy family," the Mouse said. "Noah will be lost without his sister."

"Not technically his sister," I felt compelled to point out.

The two of us stood in a neat, three-walled bedroom with a brass bed, a rocking chair (though neither of us hinged in the middle) and a round carpet, all vaguely Victorian.

"What upset Bella?" I asked. However, if anything the Mouse knew less than I.

"They had a fight. People do, sometimes. Maybe Freddy broke something. That's usually why Nora and Noah fight. Nora broke Noah's Lego helicopter after he spent so long putting it together."

"I think this was a bit more complicated, psychologically speaking," I said.

"Anyway, Noah forgave Nora. Maybe Bella will forgive Freddy. You're not in scale," the Mouse went on. "Everything here is one inch to the foot. Still, it's nice having company. Only wish it was under happier circumstances."

At seven inches I was, indeed, large for the doll house. I liked it, though, and the children's bedroom, too. I would have enjoyed watching them play together there.

"I was a birthday present when Nora turned four."

"What's Nora like may I ask?"

"She wears skirts and plays with dolls but she also loves softball. Noah's not athletic. He loves Harry Potter and Legos."

Freddy leaned into the room from the hall. "Thanks for playing so nicely while I was on the phone."

Noah, thumbs hammering away, mouth slightly open, said nothing and Freddy backed away. Later, she returned and came into the room.

"You can't do Gameboy all evening."

"Mommy reads to us."

"Okay, choose a book."

Freddy sank her substantial jeans-encased bottom into the blankets and opened the book he gave her, reading about the adventures of one Encyclopedia Brown.

"What else?" she asked, Frisbeeing the book onto a pillow.

Noah slipped off the bed and came to squat in front of the doll house.

"I've never played with dolls," Freddy said. "I'm not sure I know how."

"I found a man." He pointed at me, then at the mouse. "They're married."

"A man can't marry a mouse."

Noah stood. "No."

He returned to the bed and curled up again with his electronic plaything.

"I'm kidding. Come on, show me how to play."

"Not without Nora."

Freddy sighed and continued to sit there, staring out, while the boy played.

"What if Bella and Freddy never make up?" the Mouse asked me. "He needs his sister. She needs him."

"She's not his sister."

"Those children belong together."

"Noah and Nora have about as much power over their destinies as you or I."

A week or perhaps ten days later, Freddy came in, beaming, "Guess who's here for a play date?"

Noah's comic book fluttered to the floor as he crawled out of the lower bunk. Nora walked in past Freddy, a good six inches taller than Noah, in a short pink dress, striped leggings and dirty white sneakers.

Freddy lingered in the doorway. "Did Mommy say anything when she dropped you off? Like, about me? Think she misses me?"

"I don't know."

"Bet she misses her garden," Freddy said, heartily.

After Freddy withdrew, Nora said, "It looks the same," picking up a stuffed tiger on the bed and throwing it down again. She eyed the half-made Lego helicopter on the floor, then approached the doll house.

"I found the old man," Noah told her.

"He's too big for the mouse."

"They're married. Okay?"

"Okay. And they adopt Harry Potter."

She galloped to the Legos box and back with a tiny, oddly square plastic boy, setting him on the round carpet between the Mouse and myself.

"You like living with Gramma?"

"No. Mommy and Gramma yell a lot. You like living alone with Momo?"

"No. She sits in the dark and drinks beer."

Nora dropped down on the floor, crossing her pink-and-purple striped legs. "We need to fix this helicopter."

Noah knelt beside her. "I know."

For a moment, we three—tall old man, tiny boy, and mouse—were quiet in our miniature bedroom, then the Mouse said, "He's not in scale. Much too small. Still, I've always longed for a son."

"I think I have, too," I said.

"Bollocks," said the little plastic boy. "Yer not me mum. And yer not me dad, either."

The children lay on the floor on their elbows, Noah pawing through gray cubes, black bars and flat red squares, while Nora studied the instructions.

"We need two gray cubes with four bumps each."

An hour or so later, Freddy's shadow fell over the children, the light in the hall behind her.

"It's good to see you guys playing together. I missed that." The children looked up at her from the floor. "If

Mommy could see you guys..."

She came in and sat heavily on the bottom bunk. Her eyes looked blurred. Perhaps she was tired, working too hard.

"So, Nora, I'm out of the loop here. Maybe you can help. I hear Mommy has a new friend. That true?"

"Mommy has lots of friends."

"Right. So, does this friend sleep over?"

"No."

"Really? Cuz this guy at work said–"

"—Mommy goes to her house."

"And leaves you?"

"With Gramma. Mommy and Gramma need time apart, Mommy says."

"Fuck."

Noah laughed, looking at the Lego pieces in his hand.

Freddy stood and came toward the doll house, kneeling with a grunt.

"Here's a nice little family scene. Only three, though. Is this guy an only child?"

She picked up Harry, talking in a high voice, "Where's my sister? I want my sister. Did the dragons take her?"

In a deeper voice, Freddy said, "We don't know, son."

Then, in her real voice, Freddy said, "Christ, my hand looks old."

Dropping Harry onto his side, she got up, hand braced on thigh. With a wave to the children, she walked out of the room.

"Momo's weird." Noah, cross-legged on the floor, spun the plastic helicopter propeller with his index finger.

"Next time you come to Gramma's."

"I heard that." Freddy lurched round in the hall. "What's so bad about being weird? And what's that crap about 'next time Gramma's?'"

She stood with her arms apart, hands gripping the door frame, leaning into the room. "Mommy and Nora belong here. I'm going to make sure they come home soon. Know what? Mommy once said that when I want to do something I go out and do it."

She backed away. Moments later, loud music began thumping in the living room.

"That bitch left me on my side," Harry Potter said, lying on the little round carpet at my feet.

"Why don't you try magic?" said the Mouse.

"Abracadabra. Hocus pocus. Alakazam." He was silent. "If yer me mum and dad, why can't one of you set me straight?"

"Be patient, son, one of the children will set you straight soon enough."

"Because yer not me my mum and dad, that's why. We're not a family."

"Of course we are. Don't upset your mother."

My definition of family has become

50

more flexible. Now that I've seen Noah and Nora together I know that they are family, too.

Later, the music switched off mid thump. At the sound of the front door opening, the children both stood.

"Come on, pumpkin." A bulky leather bag hung from Bella's shoulder. A large pair of sunglasses sat atop her thick black hair. "Let's make like a banana."

"No rush," said Freddy. "You guys can go get a Popsicle out of the freezer first."

The children ran away, all legs and stocking feet.

"When you see the two of them together..." Freddy stared at Bella, while Bella studied the Legos on the floor.

"I know. I promise I'll never keep them apart."

"You made a promise to me once before, when we stood on that cliff near Carmel. I thought it was forever."

"We had a good thing."

"Until, what, kids messed it up? Are you serious? These kids are forever, like it or not. They're real. They bind us together, Bella."

"You're so controlling."

"Controlling?" Freddy clamped a hand on Bella's face, thumb and fingers sinking into Bella's soft cheeks, wrenching Bella's face toward hers. "My fate is in your hands. I don't even know what's going on outside of this house. I hear rumors."

The children returned, sucking on purple Popsicles. Bella ducked out of Freddy's grip. Pressing on Nora's back, she guided the little girl out of the room.

Noah followed, leaving Freddy alone.

"Shit!" Freddy's hiking boot kicked the pile of Legos, sending gray squares, white bars and red rectangles skittering across the floor. The helicopter careened onto its side, losing its propeller and part of one wall.

"Oooo, humans behaving badly," Harry said.

"Such a shame," the Mouse said.

This is what I think: I think Freddy will keep on loving Bella and do what she can to get Bella back. The rest is up to Bella. If I were Isis, I'd pray for them. As an inactive Action Figure, I can only watch and hope. Surely, a family cannot come apart as easily as a Lego helicopter. Or perhaps it can. What do I know of human behavior? I'm not a real psychiatrist. My plastic head is hollow. I'd like to make Bella return. I imagine leaping out of this doll house, ballooning to a full seven feet. But what can I do? What can any of us do?

So I say again to my new son, cursing at my feet, "Patience, Harry, patience."

———————————————————

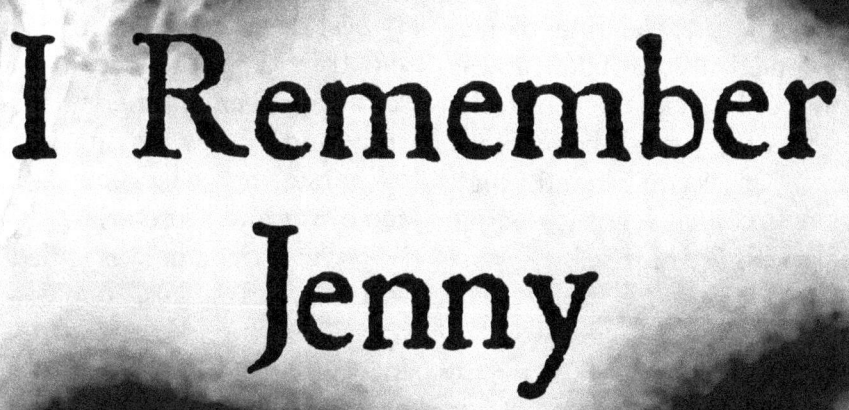

I Remember Jenny

by

Michael A. Pignatella

Herein memory, mystery, and longing...

I remember Jenny. Her fine, blonde hair trimmed like a pixie. Or was her hair long and black, thick lustrous waves? She was tiny, small-boned with fine features. Or was she tall, high cheekbones and coltish legs? It doesn't matter. The details are blurry.

But I remember Jenny.

She was nine when it happened, I think, and I was seven. It was a sticky southern New England summer, the heat and humidity setting everyone on edge, ready to snap. And that summer some folks did snap, in the form of two rival biker gangs, the Lords and the Earls, inexplicably attracted to our little city, claiming it as their own. The gangs went to war that summer, although I was only vaguely aware of it. Until the awful incident in the park.

My parents discussed it in bits and pieces of whispered conversation. Someone was dead. Crucified in the park, my father said, and I wondered if it was Jesus. But even then it was no more than a blip on my personal radar screen. It would have remained that way, if not for Jenny.

"They burned his eyes out with battery acid," she said one day, referring to the murdered biker. Her blue-brown-green eyes flared with excitement. I was the only boy in the neighborhood, my playmates all girls. My best friend, Lisa Cartin, an older girl who treated me with gentle patience, was at her grandmother's house, and so Jenny and I were playing with Jenny's toy horses, her obsession, Citation and Man o'War and Secretariat.

"My mom said he was nailed to a tree with railroad spikes," Jenny said. She capered a horse across the cracked sidewalk, while I knelt, watching, trying to imagine the murdered biker.

"We should go see where it happened," Jenny said. The idea hung there like a heavy, overripe fruit. I didn't answer. "We should go see it," she said again.

"My mother would kill me," I said.

Jenny smiled. "Okay." But it wasn't over. We played with the horses a while longer, re-enacting races, the Kentucky Derby, the Preakness. She stopped again and looked at me.

"Want to go to their house?" she asked.

"Who's house?" I asked.

"The Lords' house. It's close by, my brother says. We could peek in. It'll be an adventure." I wanted to say no, but Jenny was so pretty. As I started to shake my head, her mouth pursed into a little "o" of disappointment, and I relented.

"Sure," I said, and we went.

We rode our bikes, my white Huffy racing alongside Jenny's purple Barbie bike, sparkly tassels streaming from her handlebars. Or was it a pink bike with a red banana seat? It doesn't matter.

I remember Jenny.

We left our housing complex, riding onto Elbert Avenue, a main road, forbidden to me by my parents. It was magical, exciting, transgressive. It was dangerous, too, and I knew it. I just didn't know how dangerous.

I didn't think we'd find it, but we did. At least, we found a house. It could have been the Lords' gang house. It was a huge old Victorian, built when New Wales was still a thriving city, its forefathers still proud of what they had created. The Victorian had seen better times, the smudged white paint faded and peeling like leprosy, the windows dusty and dirty. No one seemed to live there.

"This is it, this is the place," Jenny said, her skin smooth and pale. Or perhaps dark and exotic.

"How do you know?" I asked. My hands kneaded the grooved, plastic grips on the end of my handlebars.

"I just do." Her words were convincing. She was like a dousing rod, attuned to adventure. Or magic. She walked her bike down the sidewalk to the front door. I wanted to run home, but didn't.

Dusk was settling and I wondered how long we had been gone. It was dinnertime and my mother would be worried. But my concerns were overwhelmed by Jenny, by the vividness of her reality. When she beckoned me to follow, I did.

I left my bike on the sidewalk and ran to her. She smiled and then she too dropped her bike to the ground. We walked to a big bay window set to the right of the doorway, trampling through the shrubbery growing along the front of the house, wild and untended.

Did anyone see us that day? Did anyone look out their window and see two kids, on their tippy-toes, peering into the grimy windows? Did they see Jenny, her face pressed against the glass, straining to look into what we thought was a dangerous world? Did

"The people inside. The cool people." Cool people. Like movie stars. Or gods. But I didn't get it.

they consider intruding upon our little fantasy and stopping us?

If they did, they didn't act upon it. Instead our fantasy intruded upon us.

"Do you see them?" Jenny asked. I was a good four inches shorter than her, and was having trouble seeing anything. But I wanted to please her and those big blue-green-brown eyes and so I nodded.

"Yes," I said, although all I could see was dirt and filth and multiple shades of brown.

"I can't believe it," she said. "They're wonderful. So beautiful." What was she talking about? I stepped on a small white boulder protruding from the ground, but my battered Converse All-Stars slipped, unable to purchase a grip. I grasped the window sill to steady myself. Jenny turned.

"They want us to come in," she said.

"Who?"

"The people inside. The cool people." Cool people. Like movie stars. Or gods. But I didn't get it.

"Who, the Lords?" I asked. "We can't go in there. They might crucify us or something. We should go home."

She looked at me with a look I would later realize was sympathy. "Not the Lords," she said in a quiet voice. She backed away from the window and started toward the front door. I stared at the back of her pink t-shirt (or was it blue?). She turned.

"Are you coming?" she asked, and my heart said yes. But my head said no.

She stepped up to the old, wooden door, and held her hand out in a fist, knocking once. I should have done something, screamed for help like my mother told me to do if approached by a stranger, but I didn't. It didn't seem right.

Did the door open? Was there a figure in the darkened entryway, cloaked in a white robe? Did it hold out a hand, and did Jenny take it, looking at me one last time, beckoning with her sad eyes, then entering the house, leaving me alone? I don't know. I remember it happening. But memories are ephemeral things.

I biked home. My tires whirred over the sidewalk, cutting through the haziness of the dusk and the buzzing of the electric lines overhead. Fear, palpable, like snot coating my throat, threatened to choke me.

Jenny had been kidnapped. I remembered something she had said to me one time about kidnappers, while we played with her horses. "They put Popsicle sticks in your privates," she said. That thought saturated my mind as I pedaled, convinced it was true. I biked faster.

Nothing looked familiar. I was lost, and thought I would never find my way home. But then the sound of my mother's voice, high-pitched and on the verge of panic, reached my ears, and I headed toward her. When I pedaled out of the darkness into her vision, her knees seemed to buckle in relief.

"Where in God's name were you?" she asked, even as she swept me off my bike, letting it clatter to the ground. "I can't believe you would take off like that. Your father is out driving around looking for you. . ." She looked into my eyes.

"Are you okay? Did something happen?" She shook me with a ferocity that snapped me out of my haze.

"Jenny's been kidnapped," I said, and I could tell she didn't believe me. Then I told her the details, told her about looking for the Lords' hideout, about the house, about how Jenny went in.

"Let's get home, now," she said in a hard voice. We headed off, my mom running alongside my bike. She made two calls as soon as we arrived.

One to Jenny's mother. The other to the police.

They never found her. Jenny's snatching was a huge story, gracing the front cover of the New Wales Journal-Enquirer for weeks. And I was the co-star in that drama, the survivor. The lucky one.

I tried to help the police, but it was hopeless. A police officer drove me in his cruiser, looking for the neighborhood where Jenny had disappeared. When I told him we had been at the Lords' hideout, the policeman, Officer Tartleton, looked at me with a gentle smile and said, "There is no Lords' hideout, son. At least none I'm aware of. You'll have to show me where you were."

So we set off, but I couldn't remember where the house was, my memory addled by fright and confusion. I've never been good with directions. We drove up side streets and main roads, past older homes and newer subdivisions, until finally I thought we had found it.

"Right there," I said, pointing to a Victorian made visible in the gloom by its lone porch light. We approached the home together (to this day I'm amazed Officer Tartleton didn't make me stay in the cruiser), and as we moved closer I realized something was wrong. This home wasn't abandoned. It had freshly painted dark green shutters and clean windows. I could see a television through one, the Red Sox playing in Fenway Park. Officer Tartleton rang the doorbell.

"Can I help you?" said the man who answered, and he didn't look like a kidnapper at all. He was tall and thin, wearing a blue t-shirt that said "Salty Dog Café" and gray athletic shorts. He was barefoot, and looked surprised.

"Yes, sir, I'm sorry to bother you," began Officer Tartleton, and I could tell he didn't think this was the right house. It was. And yet it seemed nothing like the house we had found. Peering behind the man, I could see pictures on the wall, a sofa, a coffee table with a tin of Jiffy Pop on it. Could I have been wrong?

Then I saw her, in the archway between the living room and the kitchen. She had red hair and too-big green eyes, as if her pupils were straining to absorb all the available light. A swath of scarlet freckles danced across her otherwise pallid skin. She looked nothing like Jenny. But it was her.

"There she is," I said and Officer Tartleton looked down at me. He had already put away his notebook and was making small talk about the Red Sox.

"Who?" he asked.

"Jenny." I pointed into the home, past the man at the door, who looked at me with a smile that made my skin itch.

"I'm sorry, son," the man said, "but you're mistaken. That's my daughter, Karen. Come here hon."

The girl approached. She wore a green t-shirt and jean shorts, and I thought I might be mistaken. Then I saw the toy horse, a broad Chestnut, Secretariat, clutched in her small hands, and knew I was right.

I remember Jenny.

"That's not your daughter," I said, "that's Jenny." Officer Tartleton put his hand on my shoulder.

"Calm down," he said, "I know this has been upsetting, but no use worrying others." He knelt down to the girl's height. "What's your name?" he asked.

"Karen," she said, her voice clean in the still, muggy air. In my head, she said Jenny.

"I'm sorry, sir," said Officer Tartleton to the man, and then we left, his hand firm on my back. I felt chastened, embarrassed. But it was her.

They never rescued Jenny, never returned to that house to retrieve her. I went to therapy for awhile and was declared cured. My parents wanted it that way, wanted to forget all about it. Jenny's family moved away within the year and everyone wanted to close the chapter. But I couldn't.

I saw Jenny two years later at Disney. The Florida one. Part of my therapy, the sunlight and happiness designed to erase the past. Scrubbing me like steel wool, leaving no trace of what happened. Instead, there she was.

She was with an older couple, the man graying, wearing a "World's Best Grandpa" t-shirt, plaid shorts, sandals. The woman wore a formless pink summer dress, her hair blonde, a bad dye job. They were happy, Jenny waving to Goofy, eating pink cotton candy. I stared at her, her long blonde hair, her twinkling blue eyes. Her pale blue t-shirt was decorated with a horse decal, a rearing stallion, fierce and proud. She walked past, our eyes meeting for one moment, recognition flickering and then snapping closed.

I remember Jenny.

I didn't see her again for six years or so, until tenth grade, a field trip to New York City. A Broadway musical, Brigadoon, or maybe Cats. Chinatown for dinner. My friend Mark Tardy had brought some booze, little nip bottles of Schnapps and brandy swiped from his father's bar. We drank in the back of the bus, crouched low behind the high-backed seats so our teacher, old Mrs. Galloway, wouldn't see us.

The liquor burned my stomach, the acidic taste stewing in my innards. Sick, both Mark and I struggled through the musical with cold sweats, suddenly not so cool, not so smart. But by the time we arrived at the Chinese restaurant, I was feeling a bit better. A little hungry even, despite the fact the authentic Chinese food looked nothing like the takeout back home in Connecticut.

I saw her at the restaurant, even as I stared at my soup, avoiding the little floating things that looked like eyeballs. She was Chinese, her hair long and thick and black, straight down her back. She was with a teenage boy, her boyfriend, in a table in the back corner. I thought nothing of her at first, sipping my soup, willing myself to swallow it. Then she raised her napkin to her mouth, exposing a charm necklace against her blue turtleneck. A horse charm.

It was her, Jenny, Chinese features or not. I stared at her, my soup forgotten, until she looked back. She smiled at me, and I was sure. It was the same smile, the same mischievous, happy, carefree smile. Jenny's smile. I ate nothing further, watching her, studying her until she left, gripping her boyfriend's hand. She had black nail polish on her fingertips, a silver ring on her thumb. They walked by us and she looked at me one final time.

She winked. I remember that wink, remember what it stood for, what it invited. Freedom and adventure. Then she was gone, leaving me with my sour stomach and a plate of cold food.

I remember Jenny.

She was at my senior prom. Debbie Torgleson was my date, a junior who I wasn't really dating but who had made out with me at some parties, hiding behind the haze of a six-pack of Bartles & Jaymes wine coolers. We had a fight and she stormed off to the ladies' room, her bright green prom dress trailing behind her. I could have chased her, but didn't think I needed to. It was my prom, after all, and Debbie wasn't going to ruin it. I was heading back to our table when I saw her.

Jenny, in a light blue, low-cut gown, walking toward me. It was her, even though her hair was curly and dark. When she bumped into me, I grabbed her, my arms around her waist, feeling her so close, so real, so alive. She stiffened, as if my touch offended her. Was it her? But then she leaned over, her mouth at my ear, and she whispered.

"Citation," she said, her voice barely audible in the blare of the music. Our code word. A shiver of excitement trickled down my spine, like the last drop of champagne being drained from a glass. That one word, so normal, so sensual, so personal. She backed away, her face once more a mask of anonymity. But I knew.

I remember Jenny.

I only saw her once that night, but it was enough. Later, I imagined her as Debbie and I had sex in a bedroom in Mark Tardy's parents' beach house, and I almost cried out her name when I came.

"I love you," Debbie said afterward, misunderstanding my passion, thinking it was for her.

"You're great," I responded, and Debbie's eyes dimmed. She dressed while I lay there, thinking of Jenny, and left without a word. It was a relief.

I danced with Jenny in college one night, at Charlie O's, a local bar. I was drunk, so smashed even my friends had abandoned me, and it would have only been a matter of time before a bouncer threw me out. One was approaching me as I swayed unsteadily, my face hot, my stomach sloshing. She cut in between us.

"He's with me, I'll take care of him," she said to the bouncer, a thick block of a man. He looked at her and I didn't think he would buy it, but he did, turning and hunting for easier prey.

"Thanks," I said, aware, even through my drunken haze, of the embarrassment from which she had rescued me. "Do I know you?" I asked, and she smiled. She was a redhead again, her hair up in a loose bun. Not a freckle-faced redhead, but a mature, sensual one. Auburn. Her eyes were green and they sparkled, as always.

"Dance with me," she said, and she took my hand and led me out to the dance floor. We danced, her body fluid, so natural even I could follow. I realized what other, better dancers must feel, the melding of two bodies into one. Like sex, just like people say.

We danced and the night passed, and then it was last call, the lights flashing, and I imagined her leaving with me, making love to me, letting me in on the secret. Instead, as the last song played, she pushed me against the wall and kissed me, hard, urgent, her tongue probing my mouth, and then she pulled back just as forcefully. She smiled a sad smile and left. Only when the door had closed did I feel the small business card she had pushed into my hand.

It was her. On the front of the card

was a drawing of a horse and the name, address and phone number of a local head shop, "The White Pony." On the back was her handwriting. "Call me," it said, but there was no number. I suppose she could have meant to call her at the White Pony, but I didn't. I've never been comfortable in places like that. Too wild.

I kept the card, pulling it out occasionally to look at it, to smell it, imagining I could smell her, inhale her essence. Over time, the handwriting faded, leaving a blank where her presence had been. But the memories don't fade.

I remember Jenny.

I hadn't seen her since, until this week. I was sure she would be in attendance at my wedding, smiling at me even as Laura and I exchanged vows. I couldn't have gone through with it if Jenny had been there. She wasn't at the birth of my daughters either. She left me alone, let me live my life. But I didn't forget.

She's moved next door. I watched her out my window, watched the moving van pull up, watched them unload her stuff. Weird stuff, hanging beads and psychedelic art and crap like that. I felt funny as I watched, my skin prickly, and then they unloaded the statue, a black stallion carved from what looked like obsidian, dark and muscular and alive. I knew it was her before I saw her.

She's come full circle, blonde and petite, the way I think I remember her. Ethereal. I watched her direct the movers, alone, unmarried as I knew she would be. Keeping the faith. She saw me standing in my picture window and she waved, a shy wave that belied the invitation on her face. I waved back, a raise of my hand, and then I went into the den and retrieved the business card from my desk drawer.

"Are you okay?" Laura asked when she found me, and I nodded yes. It wasn't a lie. I'm better than I've been in ages.

Laura and the girls are at the movies. I'll be gone before they return. It's been a long time, but in some ways it's like it was yesterday. I'm going over to Jenny's house, and when she answers the door I'm going to tell her I'm ready, I want to join her and the cool people, and then I'm going in.

I remember Jenny. And I won't let her forget me.

———————————————

The Kemetian
Husesen Craze

by

Edward W. Robertson

The Aether Age... Herein, circa 475 BCE

After it became declassified, I would use the trip as the setup for a joke: An Athenian and an Argive wander into a Scythian mercenary camp. Men toweled down horses, eying us beneath high-crowned hats. I gazed over the shallow, houseless valley, pretending not to listen to Philocrates pretending to sell out our homeland to the bearded Scythian chief.

As usual, I was the servant. Philocrates was the lord. His assumptions needed rearrangement.

"Good-looking piece," Philocrates said, hoisting a musket whose red-stained stock could have been carved by the same hand behind the ones we'd recovered from their raids beyond the Ister. Some third of the soldiers in camp carried them on shoulders or saddles. They all wore bows, quivers. Stitched leathers and furs. Some wrapped their feet in rags. I'd been staring; I turned up my face, caught the speck of an asteroid

about to cross the eye of the sun on its march through the aether.

"But a bitch to aim mid-gallop," the chief grinned. He nodded to a long, thick tube racked beside his tent. "Not that you need to aim all of them."

Philocrates raised his eyebrows for permission and took up the tube. He turned it, tapped it. Click of bronze. Smiled apologetically. "My man amuses himself studying the weapons of foreign lands."

Prick. I took the tube, muttered "Han" in Hellene. Philocrates nodded fractionally and returned to the subject of our troop positions. The information wasn't current, just recent enough to buy favor without paying in Hellene blood.

Long, bronze, dents down its length, scorch marks on both open ends. Smelled like saltpeter and hell. Two-thirds along, the tube sported a clamp and touch hole like an old matchlock. I nodded and eased it back onto the rack.

Philocrates prattled on. Men left to rummage the grassy hills for rabbits and tubers. Another Titan creased the sun. I'd have been done an hour ago. Philocrates turned the talk to the nomadic patterns of the chief's ancestors. When the chief paused between generations, I stepped forward, head bowed.

"Excuse me, lord. Is it possible for you to sell us one of these firing-tubes?"

64

The chief smiled indulgently. "Afraid not."

"Pity," Philocrates took up. "I imagine a few of those and we could wreak horror on the Argives."

The man chewed his beard. "Go to Olbia. Find a man named Abchadas. He'll have what you need to kill the Hellenes."

I nodded, masking my rage with a smile. A third Titan had caught the sun before Philocrates fared his wells.

We mounted and headed east across the plains. On the north shore of the Euxine, Olbia would be a week's ride if we couldn't catch an airship.

"So," Philocrates said. "Think they're reinvesting the spoils of war?"

"They don't have any money. Some of those guys don't have shoes."

"Yet they're laden with Han weaponry. What an illogical phenomenon." He brushed brown hair from his eyes. "What's the tube do?"

I shrugged. "Blow things up."

"Really? Fascinating! The Han are magicians with gunpowder, you know. I wonder if they're fire-brained by nature or by incident?"

I pulled my coat close around my shoulders. "I wonder how long before the mercenaries use those things on our people."

"Kemetian," I said, nodding to the wide-spaced ruts in the road to Abchadas' hilltop manor. "Lot of them, too, judging by the depth. Or their chariots are especially heavy."

Philocrates wound a strand of hair around his finger. "Suppose we should catch a ship for the Nile right now?"

"We still don't know how they're funding the raiders."

"But it would spare us an hour of yammering from a rich man. Like apples, they all look different on the outside, but inside, they all carry the same seed: the conviction their wealth was the natural outcome of a healthy cosmos."

"Sounds annoying." Pines and deep green shrubs furred the shoulders of the road. Whiff of the sea. How do you follow money? It doesn't leave the same tracks a man does. It isn't something you can catch, kill, and eat. Money is a notion, as liquid and hard to hold as the aether that surrounds the world and lets us reach for others.

But now I'm starting to sound like Philocrates. Too much time together.

A pair of servants in wool coats greeted us at the gates and tried to peel Philocrates away.

"Andronikos," he hissed. I examined the ironwork elk and eagles mounted on the wall, letting him twist, then waved him on. Abchadas waited for us in a hall of wrought iron and boasts.

"At last," he said through a bear's beard. "What, did you walk here?"

I smiled. "My servant's afraid of traveling on anything higher than a horse."

"He sounds easily replaced."

"More easily than he believes," I said. I doused Philocrates' glare with a look. Abchadas laughed and chatted, showing us around, voice echoing through the empty space he'd captured within his walls. I nodded when I was supposed to, praised when conversation called for praise. After a life in the military, it was second nature.

Philocrates shifted foot to foot, wandered off to eye the animal- and hero-heavy metalwork draped from the walls. I considered killing Abchadas once we had our intel; he was thin-armed and middle-aged. Not that I expected that to dam the tide of arms flowing into Scythia. The gesture was the thing.

We'd come on pretense of arranging a buy. At last, I swung to business.

Abchadas' beard ruffled as he nodded. "Follow me to the courtyard. All deals should be made under the sun."

I snapped my fingers for Philocrates. The courtyard brimmed green, interrupted by reds and yellows and blues.

"Is this your only business?" I sighted down a matchlock pistol, also Han.

"Primarily and most profitably." Abchadas smiled. "Lately I've begun to branch into gardening."

I chuckled. To Abchadas' left, Philocrates pulled a face. The Scythian spoke softly with servants who returned with smoothbore muskets and a new rifled model bearing the owl of Athens. I looked up.

"Got someplace we can give these a test?"

"Holy hells!" Philocrates shrieked from across the garden. I sprinted for him, instincts locking down thought, the slap of Abchadas' heels behind me. Philocrates bent over a waist-high yellow-stemmed plant. Lacy fronds trembled in the breeze. Shining purple petals looped in broad and tangled sprays that looked too heavy to be supported by the tender stem.

"Sir," Abchadas said, head cocked, "I'll ask you not to touch that."

"Where did this come from?" Philocrates gaped. "It's unearthly!"

"And worth two thousand owls. Don't--"

Philocrates reached for a tendril that looked soft as a sigh. Abchadas turned to me, red behind his beard.

"Sir!"

I interposed myself between Philocrates and the plant. "Back off. Or that flower won't be the only thing planted in the dirt."

Abchadas smiled tightly, eyes shining like silver drachmas. We left on the arrangement of a small deal and a false

From the open airship window, Pelousion oozed across the delta, a city of mud in a land of sand and flax. Philocrates slumped in his seat, nausea chiseled on his fine features. I smiled.

promise for more, the road unspooling toward the bay.

"Flowers," I said.

"Apparently."

"Can they get you high?"

Philocrates rubbed his mouth. "I don't believe so, although it's likely that--"

"The Kemetians are funding a literal war with flowers. At least they'll be easy to spot." I dug my heels into my horse's ribs. "We'll cable our men in Memphis. Catch an airship to Pelousion. See what there is to see."

From the open airship window, Pelousion oozed across the delta, a city of mud in a land of sand and flax. Philocrates slumped in his seat, nausea chiseled on his fine features. I smiled.

We hit the hot streets. Telegrams waited us in the mud-brick office of the local Bridge Between Two Lands cable co. Philocrates plucked them up and began decrypting.

"They're being sold up and down the Nile, but the focus seems to be Memphis." He squinted at me over his papers. "They have ferries upriver, you know."

I booked another flight.

Kemetian cities look the same to me. The same sandy bricks in Memphis as in Pelousion. Same square houses. We had a meet the next day. I toured the streets to get their feel while Philocrates roamed the markets for flowers. The faces of buildings grinned with bright murals. When I got very lucky, I whiffed lamb and cinnamon instead of shit.

The day after we headed for the fountain. On its burbling lip sat our contact Gobryas, a kronos-mooded Persian exile who hated the Kemetians even more than he hated us.

He laughed drily. "You two look like you're enjoying yourselves."

Philocrates smeared sweat from his brow. "I'm working on a theory that excessive heat leads to excessively convoluted government schemes."

"You're looking for Bes and Panhsj Botanical Endeavors," Gobryas said. "They hire day laborers on the south road every morning."

I elbowed Philocrates' ribs. "Don't worry, we'll find you some gloves."

"Unlike our quarry, I am not a

delicate flower."

Gobryas spat into the dirt. "I don't know why I'm doing this. I should just let you two peoples destroy each other."

I shrugged. "If you've seen war, you know nobody deserves it."

"Or maybe we all do."

I gave him an address to pick up his fee and we headed off for bad haircuts and shabby clothes. As we searched for a barber willing to do slipshod work ("Anyone can cut hair nicely. True artistry lies in deliberately doing so poorly," Philocrates tried to explain), Philocrates told me about a near-riot down on the docks when three of the plants had gone up for auction.

"It was as if they were bidding on a new form of gold. Or their own souls." He paused in the shade of an etched limestone lintel. "It's called the husesen, by the way."

We chopped our hair, frayed our robes, dirtied our skins. The following morning we looked no different from any of the others clustered around the south road. Possibly a mistake-- the B&P wagoner looked right past us, beckoning a half dozen others on board.

In this way we wasted a week. Afternoons, we sniffed after the husesen and turned up crumbs. Only available through B&P. Very expensive. Their origin, you may as well ask what formed the stars.

Finally, the wagoner ushered us onto the stinking boards. We rattled away from the mud-smog of Memphis. The dirt road branched, taking us to a line of boundary stones demarcating tidy green rows and empty churned dirt.

And row on row of red-headed poppies.

We harvested seeds. Clipped flowers. Hoed dirt. Dug onions. Carried water. We sweated and blistered and slapped flies. Far across the fields, beyond a wire fence, men with muskets prowled the empty space around high brick buildings.

During rests, we wandered nearer. A gleaming chariot rolled to the wire gates, garnered inspection, and entered.

"Whatever's in there," Philocrates panted, "it's not to be seen by the likes of us. Naturally, then, our coworkers will be more curious than those who work inside the building, and likely better-informed."

I doubted this. But by the second day, he introduced me to a short and wiry Kermani named Menali.

"Husesen, they inside," he said in wounded Kemetian. "A hundreds. Wall to wall."

"They grow them there?" Philocrates said.

Menali grinned the grin of a man who spots the fish beneath the surface. "No. Not grown. Brought in."

Philocrates turned to me, mouth a white line. "We're no closer--"

68

"Big ship," Menali finished. "Nobody knows when."

"I wonder what they look like," I said, misdirecting.

"That, you can't say. Do they light up in darkness? This is so I hear."

"Amazing," Philocrates said. That night on our road back to Memphis, he said, "He must have meant an airship. Just by watching its course we'll be able to narrow down its origin."

"I don't know." I rubbed my back. "Think you can make it another week?"

"I haven't been one of your pampered Assembly speakers in years. Do you keep droning on about that out of laziness? Or because your brain's still catching up?"

I didn't say much on the way back to our one-room apartment. And now a new ship to chase? An end to the journey: did it exist, now the world had grown so large?

With his usual pride, Philocrates once told me of an argument he'd had with a priest about the nature of the aether. The priest held that the invisible aether surrounding our planet, its debris ring, and the moon--and who knew how much further--was the exhalation of Zeus. Only a heavenly breath that could support us, wherever we went, as if we walked on Earth.

Philocrates countered that air, when exhaled, can't keep anyone alive, at least not very long. Yet men can breathe aether. Therefore, the aether couldn't be the exhaled air of any god, Zeus or not.

The priest replied with something about the internal working of gods differing from our own. Philocrates took that as a confession of defeat. I expect both men went home saying they'd won: Philocrates because he always does, the priest because the debate only proved a natural philosopher will ignore the grandeur of Olympus as soon as the smallest mote of logic catches his eye.

I don't know what the aether is. But I've fought enough wars to know the difference between an airship and an aethership. Airship bodies and balloons are long cylinders, fish-like, meant to cleave the seas of air. In the sky above the guarded brick building, the descending ship bore three spherical balloons over a fat and blocky gondola.

"That's no airship," Philocrates said. I cocked my head. He went on, "I crewed one in the War of Aegean Hegemony. Auxiliary strategist."

"Great. Figure out how we'll get on board."

"Now?"

"We don't know when it'll be back."

"I would propose," he said, shifting his robes on his shoulders, "we return to Memphis, cable Athens, and arrange a flight on a ship of our own."

"It's headed into the aether. We'll have no clue where it goes from there. Like trying to follow a fish through the ocean." I chunked my hoe into the soil. "You're the thinker, aren't you? We can count on two hours. Get thinking."

"What I think is you're asking me to plan our suicide."

I hefted the hoe. I think better when I'm working. Beyond the wire fence, the ship touched down in a wreath of sand and steam. Wouldn't matter too much if we bought the farm. We'd cabled Athens last night. They knew everything we did.

"Consider the aethership," Philocrates said softly some time later.

A rectangular box under three bulging spheres. Landing rails beneath the box. Stylized vulture painted on its side. "Consider it considered."

"Unlike their air and sea-going counterparts, the top deck of an aethership is closed. If a man were to climb on top of it and install himself there between it and the balloons, spotting him would be very difficult."

I blinked. Not just for the sweat in my eyes. "That's the best you can do?"

"With this little time, preparation, and resources? You're lucky I'm not asking us to cling like lemurs to the landing rails."

I grinned. A ladder tongued down from the belly of the ship to cough out crates and personnel. Men came and went. No strict security per se: guards roamed the grounds, monitored the buildings and gate, sometimes glanced shipward. Risky. Not impossible.

Unloading became loading. Time to move. We picked up buckets and headed for the stream. Knee-high grass became waist-high reeds. We left our buckets on the bank and doubled back for the fenced-off field, crouching, belly-crawling when the grasses dipped. I reached the fence and shimmied under.

A hundred yards from the ship, its balloons straining under ropes and clasps. Traffic came and went from the ladder. I swung around for the stern.

"Who's there?"

I froze. A tan arm parted the grass in front of my face. I grabbed it, yanked the man down beside me. He opened his mouth and I jammed my forearm between his teeth. He bit down, drawing blood; I jammed harder. Fingers scraped my cheeks, seeking eyes. I thrashed my head and the fingers clamped for my throat. I saw spots, flashes. Philocrates hunched behind me, gaping. The man leaned his weight over me, snot spraying from his flaring nostrils, molars grinding the meat of my arm. I reached between his legs and crushed his balls. He dropped my throat and I punched his, dropping him. I struck until his eyelids drooped.

Wind tousled the grass. Light conversation carried from the ladder. I gasped back my breath.

70

The guard carried a curved sword and single-shot pistol. I snugged them both beneath my robes. Philocrates wouldn't meet my eyes. We crawled on until the ship hung above us, a beast of wood and tin and brass, body blocking us from sight. I reached above my head, grasped the neck of an iron vulture, and hauled myself hand over hand.

I rolled onto the roof, panting. Philocrates followed moments later. If anyone saw us, they hadn't made any noise about it. We crawled to the middle and flattened down.

"That was so fast," Philocrates murmured.

I paused, clamping hands with a sudden pang of pity. "It doesn't matter how you react. All that matters is you don't do nothing."

The engines kicked on a few minutes later; my hand snaked for a rope. That big wooden body mumbled and thrummed. I tangled my legs into the cabling as the ship jerked and lifted.

I didn't risk a look until I'd counted five minutes. At the roof's lip, wind swirling my hair, the Nile peeled a vast green ribbon through a sprawl of brown and yellow. I swallowed.

Clouds wrapped us in a damp blanket. Philocrates squeezed his eyes tight. I pulled my robes tight against the leeching chill. The clouds ebbed to nothing. Beyond the great, steaming bubbles, the sky darkened like the water

beyond an undersea cliff, first a perfect blue, then a star-pricked, twinkling blackness. As we moved from air to aether, the bone-cold subsided for an uneasy cool.

The engines hushed. My limbs, when I shifted, moved as lightly as if I were swimming. I jerked against the feeling of falling, propelling myself into a tangle of ropes.

"What in Hades?"

"Hold tight!" Philocrates said, hair billowing around his head. "As matter is by nature drawn to other matter, the Earth's grip slackens as you leave its mass behind. We won't feel that hold again until we reach another body."

I squirmed, palms sweating, hauling my weightless body back for the solid wood roof. I glimpsed the world, whorls of white over sweeps of blue and green. Something in that vision calmed me. A deep terror, too, but so deep I could give in, knowing I'd have no way to fight.

I focused on my breathing. If my body knew a difference between aether and air, I couldn't feel it.

Hours later a new body swelled beyond the curves of the balloons, a patch-haired thing of green and gray. The sky tilted and I swallowed down my breakfast. The ship swung through what felt like half an arc, impossible to tell, before steadying and venting great gouts of steam. The grasp of weight resumed, first light as silk, then a firm but fractional hold.

I glared at Philocrates. "You didn't tell me it would be like this."

"I thought nothing was too rough for your calloused experience."

The ship jarred down, clacking my teeth shut. More steam, thumps and hollers from the cabin beneath us. The balloons sagged like the muscles of a dead deer; would they suffocate us? The ship rocked. Voices rang through the open aether now, oddly hollow.

I waited for the last man to fade into silence before I rose. Crazed plants sprang from the dirt, broad-leafed, pale green and deep yellow. Some stretches lay barren. Rocky and empty as the crown of a mountain.

Philocrates narrowed his eyes. "One of the Titans. Hyperion, gauging by its curve. Locating the husesens here could be a complicated task."

"If they're here at all." Nobody stirred the meadow below. I climbed down effortlessly, landed with a pat. I hadn't seen where the crew had gone. Tracks led everywhere. I bared my teeth and headed for the vague direction where the voices had departed.

The grass plunged into a sweet-smelling bog. We splashed forward, parting man-high reeds. Footprints here and there. I hacked at clogging bushes, their nimble branches self-woven like a tangled net. Abruptly, the land sloped into a jungle of weeds and flowers. Arm-

thick stems supported heads as broad as barrels. Blues, purples, blacks, specks and streaks of yellows and reds and whites.

I lost the trail. Now and then what I hoped was a breeze rustled the petals and leaves. I doubled back, found nothing. The crush of plants screened out the sky.

"Are we lost?" Philocrates whispered.

"We need to find a hill."

That took doing. By the time we emerged from the flowering forest to a bare ridge, the Earth hung beside the sun in the black sky. Night fell with the swiftness of a bird.

I scanned the darkened land. No fires, no lights. "I'm out of my element, Philocrates."

"All lands look foreign to virgin eyes. Look, there's a light just over there."

I followed his arm. Less than a mile away, a prick of light appeared from a shadowy meadow. It brightened as I watched, joined by others.

"Mark the direction," I said. "And be quiet."

We climbed down into a new forest that soon broke into a flat plain of grass. Patches glowed like stolen moonlight.

"See any houses?" I said. "Any people?"

I got out the pistol and crouched forward. I don't know who stopped first. Yellow-stemmed, purple-fronded husesen spread above the grass, spilling silvery light across the plain.

"Xenophytes!" Philocrates laughed. "I knew it!"

He bounded forward. I kept watch while he made notes, harvested seeds, took clumsy clippings. Beyond the flowers' glow, I squinted stones rising from the gloom. Ruins. When I pointed them out, Philocrates bounded off like a wind-up toy. Crumbled walls bore foreign glyphs and figures, too timeworn to make out. Beside them lay a wide and well-trampled landing field and a narrow building of fresh stone covered in Kemetian murals. In its courtyard loomed a monstrous wheeled engine of wood and rope. A long arm extended from its center, straining beneath its cocked tension, a sling dangling from its end. The unblinking Earth gazed with us.

"That," I said, "is an enormous catapult."

Despite the clear Kemetian presence, we found no one inside the building. Desks and papers, which Philocrates took to like the proverbial moth. I poked around, found a warehouse of aethership tackle, sat down on a bundle of canvas to rest my eyes.

"Andronikos!"

I jolted awake. Early dawn filtered throw the slitted windows. I rushed to the study, sword in one hand, pistol in the other. Philocrates rushed toward me and waved a handful of papers in my face.

"The catapult! They mean to bombard us with it!"

"You're sleep-mad. Even if they could fling something free of the Titan's grip, it would wind up on the other side of the planet."

"The Earth's face hasn't changed since we've been here. It's as if this asteroid's locked in place." His red eyes bulged. "A normal catapult can knock down walls. What do you think would happen if they launched a boulder from here?"

Natural philosophers. "I've worked with artillery. They couldn't hit the Aegean from here, let alone a city."

"If they keep working on this, they'll find a way."

A man with a shaved head and white robe leaned through the doorway, blanched, and disappeared. I ran after him while Philocrates stuffed papers in his robe. Men shouted in Kemetian from the landing field. A small ship rested a couple hundred yards away, still venting steam.

"We should run," I said.

"To hide up here eating alien flowers?" Philocrates' eyes swung toward the catapult. He giggled. "Did you see any cloth in there? Big cloth. Something you could make a sail out of."

"There's a room full of rigging and

supplies off the study."

His eyes and mouth rounded. "Hold them off! Don't let them near the machine!"

He sprinted inside. Across the field, men scrambled in and out of the ship. Steel flashed. A lone musket crashed, echoing through the ruins. I knelt and rested my firing arm across a rock.

There's always a brave one. A man in a loincloth rushed from the ship, a curved blade glinting over his head. I let him get within twenty feet, shot him in the chest, and collected his sword from the grass. In response, a half dozen advancing soldiers dropped prone and began sniping from the grass. Smoke billowed from their barrels. A ball bounced from my stone cover with a dumb whine.

"Put this on!" Philocrates emerged from the building clutching two strapped packs to his chest. He hurled one at me. In the low weight, I had to leap to snag it from the air. "Come on. Now."

He raced for the catapult in long strides. I broke cover. Shouts and shots replied across the field. Philocrates jumped for the machine's long arm, clung to it, and clambered into the slack sling.

"Get in!"

For a moment, I forgot all about the armed men rushing our way. "We'll be dashed across Attica!"

"I'm not doing nothing! Trust me and get in here, you thoughtless loaf!"

I made my peace and jumped for the sling. Philocrates grabbed my arm, hauling me inside with a strength he'd never have on Earth. He snatched my sword and swung it at the machine's pin. The wooden creak, the bodily jolt: I don't know which assaulted me harder.

We sailed into empty space.

Smoke puffed below us, futile parting shots. Philocrates pounded me on my shouldered pack, grinning like a drunk on his birthday. "Parachutes. Standard issue on military airships. If we handle ourselves right, we may land in a friendly place."

"If I'd eaten in the last day, I'd be vomiting right now."

"Oh, I brought some husesen seeds, too. Kemet won't have its monopoly for long." His glee melted into troubled pensivity. "We'll have to come up here ourselves, you know. Build our own platforms. The only way to dissuade Kemet will be to convince them we can respond in kind."

"I don't like where that thought leads me."

Philocrates equivocated, then launched into a lecture on the proper operation of a parachute. Earth soared above us --or did it rest below?-- ready to take back its two unlikely birds.

74

Hail Caesar: Creative Commons and the Small Press

"It is not these well-fed long-haired men that I fear, but the pale and the hungry-looking."
--Julius Caesar

---

1. Write story
2. Get said story published
3. Profit! Karma!

I believe short fiction is important. The small press magazine I edit (Fantastique Unfettered, aka FU) uses a Creative Commons license, CC-BY-SA*, for reasons related to this view, and in service to the dual end-goals of money and karma on behalf of the writers we publish.

Traveler illustration by M.S. Corley, from
The Aether Age: Helios.

Our alignment is not indie against corporate, small against large, or fan against pro. Those are foolish stances. Our alignment is one against obscurity**, expressed via a pragmatism that acknowledges money may or may not follow our good karma. We certainly hope it does: our goal, after providing quality fiction to our readers, is to pay writers professional rates.

This article will appear in the second issue of FU, but I hope it's not where you originally read it. You see, it carries the same CC-BY-SA license. A Creative Commons, Attribution, ShareAlike license, meaning that others can do pretty much anything they want with the article, but they must give attribution and release under the same. Each instance of a presentation, adaptation, or derivative of the article is, essentially, a finger pointed back at FU. Um, not that finger.

The old world-think of walled gardens and content farms suggests the only way forward is copyright extensions, possibly to perpetuity. Our old-thinkers recognize the current audience is merely the first audience. It's a numbers game, and while individual creators will not make much to crow over statistically, the bulk IP of the mass of creators certainly will. These Caesars would own human culture, every song a commercial jingle, every myth protected by a (tm).

I'm not an ideologue: I've stated in blog posts that I don't know how well CC-BY-SA

The Aether Age & Fantastique Unfettered authors share their thoughts...

I have to admit I didn't feel good about the Creative Commons license at first, mostly I think because it is not widely used in the field or at least not that I'm aware. However, [[the FU staff]] did a good job explaining the whole thing.

~Alexandra Seidel

I love Creative Commons; I release my own work under a similar attribution share alike license once a year as part of the Homeless Moon chapbook. It's about getting my writing under as many eyeballs as possible. Nobody can make a living writing short fiction these days, and that's not what I'm in it for. I want to be read, and Creative Commons only makes that easier.

~Michael J DeLuca

I've always been drawn to live theater. At its best, the give-and-take between performer and audience creates a resonance, energizing the performance. By contrast, books have always been static.

With Creative Commons, one can choose to blur the author/reader dividing line as much, or as little, as one wants. If one uses it to break the fourth wall, the reader can become the remixer, the screenplay adaptor, or the soundtrack composer. In a digital age, it makes sense to seek new equilibriums, tailored to each situation.

~Cliff Winnig

I chose to submit to Aether Age only because of the experimental CC-BY-SA aspect of it. I had just started writing fiction after more than a decade of doing everything but, and I certainly wouldn't have spent the time immersing myself into a completely new shared world without that interesting concept of setting the story free.

~Regan Wolfrom

scales, and for the Stephen Kings of the world, traditional copyright may be the only reasonable default for their work. Creative Commons is a tool, in a toolbox that includes tradition copyright, and I have no prohibition against the latter (though even if I reach 'rock star' level, I would ensure my work returns to the culture at some point.)

With Aether Age (our first CC-BY-SA project, a shared world of space-faring Greeks and social revolutions in Egypt) we've made the work immediately available to the culture. The same is true of FU. The same will be true of my novella, Elegant Threat, to be release in the M-Brane Double #1 later this year. The New People by Alex Jeffers, the other half of the Double, will carry a traditional copyright. My first novel may carry a traditional copyright, depending on the publisher.

Writers deserve to be paid for their work, and we hope that you, dear reader, will take an active interest in supporting short fiction. If not FU then some other venue. As a writer I hope to someday make loads of cash at my craft and to have people bemoan my place on the NYT list. That hack, they'll complain as I laugh my way to the bank. (Yeah, it's a writer thing.) So, a final reminder that our use of Creative Commons licensing is not purely ideological or a revolt against traditional publishing.

Creative Commons licensing does not rob writers of ownership of their work, the ability to publish it in anthologies, collections, or even to waive the license to accommodate incoming requests to publish/adapt under other terms.

The license is a tool to reach readers, and to proclaim cultural relevance to the future. Maybe our work, and work like it, becomes an island of open/libre culture in a future of copyrighted IP masquerading as culture. We intend to run FU much like a nonprofit (though it isn't a nonprofit), to not profit off the periodical ourselves, but to use any incoming funds to make FU self-sustaining, then better pay our contributors.

CC-BY-SA is a tool for proactively freeing art to the culture, and will be right for some projects, and wrong for others. It is a tool for generating karma and reaching more readers. The other CC licenses and traditional copyright are also valid tools.

While the small press is a valuable part of the greater cultural ecosystem, big publishers (and big writers) are our heroes. Copyright is, ultimately, agnostic, insofar as it allows creators and their families to benefit from their work. The same is true of Creative Commons, and use of CC licenses does not preclude profitability.

It would be easy to stop there, with that pithy statement ignoring the real challenge we face in obscurity. The small press is a playground for the new, the odd, the possibly non-commercial --or not commercial right now--, the niche. The small press bears the responsibility to pursue the mandates of a given niche while striving for a quality of content, presentation, and a dedication to the idea

I was excited to write a story under Creative Commons Attribution Share-Alike terms. I thought it would be fun to see if my characters planted a seed in someone else's mind and lived on in a different incarnation. Film and drama are collective arts. Why not a little bit of fiction? I wouldn't want everything I write to be CC, but a short story? Sure!

~Theresa Crater

I wrote "Soybean" for the thrill, delight and entertainment value of creating a work of art. Art of art's sake. If you are writing with a specific venue/editor/publisher in mind, the work will be something less than that. Creative Commons practically screams art for art's sake, and so it is fitting that so pure a piece as "Soybean" appear under that auspice.

~J. Michael Shell

Alexandra Seidel, Michael J DeLuca, and J. Michael Shell have work in the premier issue of Fantastique Unfettered, published by M-Brane Press, and available through leading distributors such as Ingram, Baker & Taylor, Barnes & Noble, Amazon.com, Powell's, and others.

Cliff Winnig, Regan Wolfrom, and Theresa Crater have stories in the first book of The Aether Age Codex, The Aether Age: Helios, available from Hadley Rille Books. Hadley Rille Books titles are available through several distributors including Ingram, Baker & Taylor, Follett, and more. Hadley Rille Books titles are also available directly from the Publisher. Please email for more information, or to set up an order: contact@hadleyrillebooks.com.

that if anyone should be hungry and unsatisfied with imitation and shallowness, the merely commercially viable, it is us.

To close on a theme, perhaps our Caesar is that societal voice addressed to those who would participate in the culture, that suggests: you are a consumer, only.

We have come not to praise Caesar, but to bury him.

Please steal this article and post anywhere you like, just provide attribution and keep it under the same license. Encourage others to do the same.***

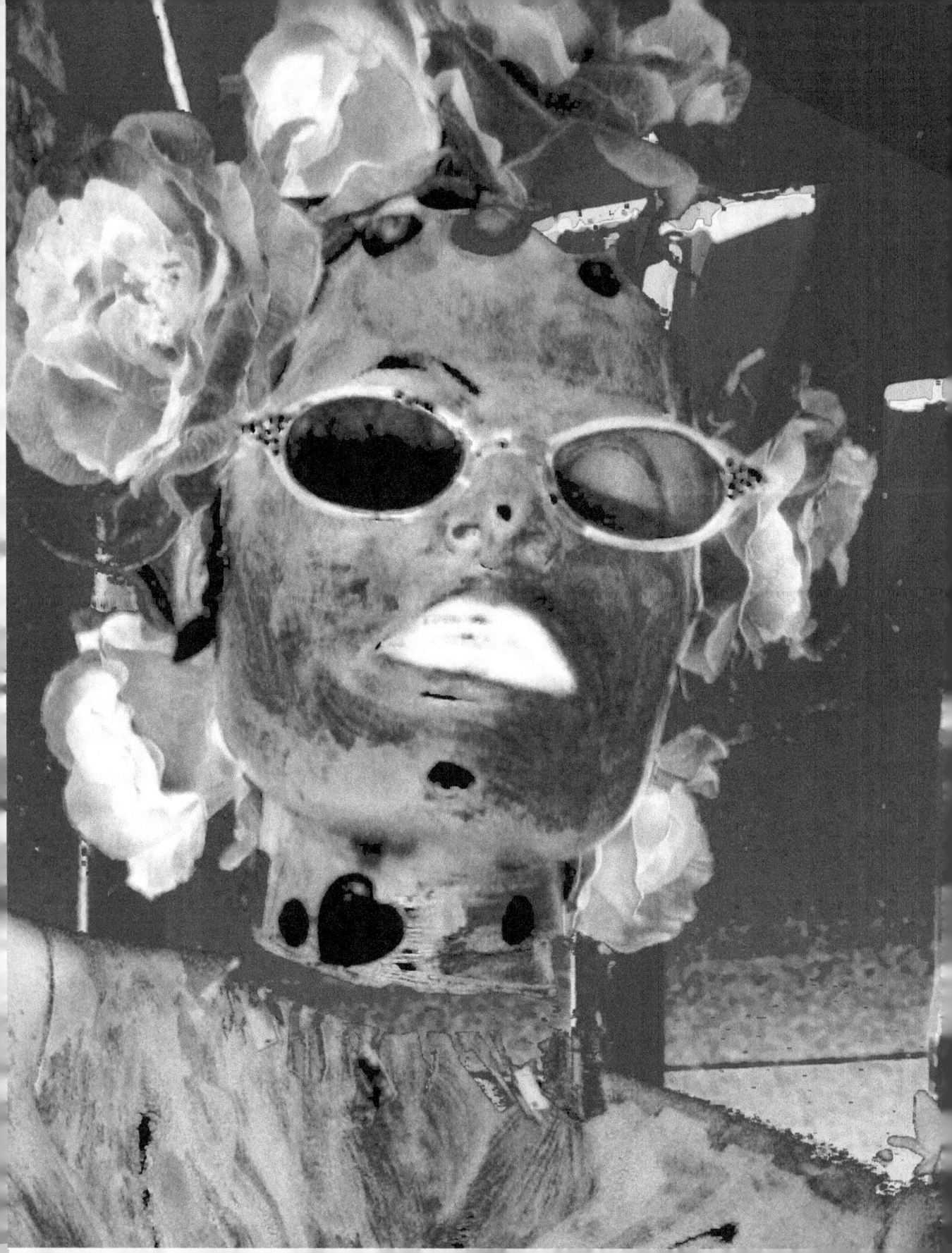

Glorious Madness

by

Jude-Marie Green

Herein. Romance and illusion... delusion...

I swear on what honor I have managed to scrape together over the past few years that she is unhinged.

Her name is Donna Quick and she is quite mad.

Myself, I am not mad. I am perhaps far too sane to spend my life following the lead of this peculiar swordswoman, but this is what I do. I am Jane Smith, magician, traveler, occasional trouble-maker. Occasionally trouble found me; and this was how I found Donna Quick, in the midst of my troubles.

The whole tale of the ugliness surrounding my introduction to her service is best suited for another time. Suffice to say she threw herself into the fray, mindless of the danger to her own person, when I was attacked by an army of ferric cats set upon me by the evil enchantress Altisidora. Her sword danced and iron cat heads flew shedding rusty fur in a splattered monochrome arc accompanied by the music of flung bells and cat screechings.

Donna Quick saved my life that night.

This was many years ago; any debt between us has been settled long past my memory; now I followed her because in all truth I loved her.

In her service I grew used to sleeping out of doors, around a campfire, with only Nature as a constant. Still I found it difficult to sleep, even after all these years, and more difficult than that to awaken each morning. As usual, on this morning Donna rose while the birds still slept. Her warmth in our blankets faded and I stirred, chilled.

I learned long ago not to ask her back into my embrace. She believes me a sluggard and has more times that I can count come after me with the flat of her sword to beat me out of my comfort. I pretended to sleep a little longer but she knew I was awake, I could see the attentive angle of her head as she moved about more noisily.

Despite my slowness, I was not slothful. Donna and I had different biorhythms. Our bodies reflected our differing humors as well. I was large enough that my leather breeches wore out in embarrassing places on a regular basis and my corset functioned overtime to strap down my mammary bits. Donna, on the other hand, never found preconstructed leathers small enough for her slight, lanky frame. Her riding gear was hand-fashioned by whatever craftswomen we met along the way.

On her own Donna would perhaps be naked. She would certainly starve to death.

I stuck my arm out from under my blanket and pointed in the general direction of the fire pit.

"Accendō," I muttered. The fire agreeably flared into existence.

When the clearing held enough warmth to melt the rimes of frost from the stones surrounding the fire pit, I threw off my blankets and stretched. From our saddlebags I gathered the necessaries for our meal: water and coffee, bread and sausage.

"Come along, your breakfast," I said, holding out a tin plate of hot food for her. She seized the plate and retreated to the far side of the fire pit.

Afterwards, I washed up and packed the camp. I could have accomplished the tasks with a few magical gestures, but I did not want to start the day worn out. Travel was exhausting enough. Before long Donna finished her morning exercises with her rapier, those swooshings with her sword that kept her the best swordswoman I'd ever known. To me her movements looked like she engaged in tango with a slim metal partner, or perhaps flamenco, some wild Spanish dance that left her and her blade sweaty and satisfied. Afterwards she wiped the blade til it gleamed then slipped it into her intricate dyed-leather scabbard.

Our mounts awaited us.

I rode an Asian designed rice-burner, soberly black, carefully polished so rust had no chance of eating her alive. The grain in the fuel nacelles murmured as I seated myself, knocking the kickstand up. I twisted the throttle and she started right up, the pleasant thrum of her single cylinder engine a nice salute to the morning.

Donna's mount, Rosinante, was of an entirely different breed. What breed that might be, I did not know. Her fuel nacelles were curved and unpainted, gray as morning fog. Her handlebars were long and drooped alarmingly towards the leather and cloth patchwork seat. Her fairings were baroque designs of swirled metal with holes poked through from some attempt at decoration that looked like a teenager's acne scars. In short, Donna's mount was the ugliest thing I had ever laid eyes on.

Yet Donna loved it and it responded with deep-voiced power that ran so

> Myself, I am not mad. I am perhaps far too sane to spend my life following the lead of this peculiar swordswoman, but this is what I do.

efficiently I swore she fed it air. If I had not known better I would have thought Rosinante an enchanted mount. But it was metal and immune to magicks.

Some time after we set off on our road I spied the first road sign of the day. Depending from the horizontal arm of a tree growing too near the common way, the painted tin sign announced that we would arrive in Wadi Seco "soon." Claims were made as to the town's lively tavern and fabulous dining possibilities.

Donna swerved as she passed the sign. She down-shifted; the roar of her mount softened to a purr and Donna put her foot down on the asphalt.

"Jane, fetch me a mirror!" Her voice was harmonic and rich in timbre. If I were blind I would still love her for just that voice. She did not consider the difficulty of producing a mirror or the incongruity of wanting it now whilst we traveled along the main road.

I complied without objection.

I sorcelled a mirror for her, as I did not carry one in my saddlebags. What would be the point of that? A mirror shivered by the vibrations of travel was no mirror at all, merely a collection of destroyed potential.

She spied herself in my impromptu magic and grunted in satisfaction at the reflected vision from my heart: bronzed willowy body, masses of golden curls, eyes the color of Argentine emeralds, and dimples meant for capturing hearts.

In truth, a truth I tended to disregard, her hair was gray and wiry with wind; her eyes faded from too many years of betrayed hope and misplaced trust. Her skin was the slick leather of someone with too many miles totaled in the accounting book of her days. But still she gleamed, oh yes, especially when she was preparing to embark upon some new mischief.

This morning she was fairly luminescent.

"Jane, I have the desire for some civilized company, some cold drink and hot food and games of chance. In short, I want to stop at this tavern and sit in on a game of veintiuna."

Her desires announced, she started up her mount again and sped onto the road. I hurried to catch up.

Some time in a village, soft beds and clean sheets, appealed to me, but we had little money, perhaps just enough to stretch for the evening. Of course Donna Quick might smooth the way for us financially. She was good at card games if not the best player I'd ever known. She might make us a stake, she might not. Either way, a day of taverning and a night of comfort seemed a good way to break our travels.

Not an hour later, the crash of the gaming table turned topsy interrupted my fledgling flirtations with a gentleman at the bar.

86

The warm looks he sent my way from the moment we entered this tavern made me moist with possibility. The road had been long since our last laying-by, and my mount's seat, pleasant though it can be, grew stale as a source of pleasure. He was handsome enough, tallish, not too muscular, dark curly hair and blazing brown eyes, a hawk's nose and the kind of lips that promised sensual pleasures. Over a draft of beer I learned his name: Miguel; and he learned mine. I enjoyed the way my name sounded on his lips.

"Who is your companion?" he said, his hand brushing my arm.

"Her name is Donna Quick," I murmured. Then I heard the harsh rise of voices from her gaming table and I sighed.

"Her name is Donna Quick and she is quite mad."

I said this as a litany against terror and perhaps as a prayer to all the gods that she would not get us murdered. It occurred to me that I have earnestly prayed this same phrase many times before.

The tavern, this anonymous establishment in a forgettable town on the road to someplace better, filled with silence. Men and women stood or sat motionless, barely breathing, containing coughs and sneezes so as not to draw my mistress' attention.

For she was mad but she was also quick.

Her blade was busy etching the clothes off the back of a card playing man.

Moments before she and five identically sleazy men had sat round a table, playing some version of some card game, pinochle, bridge, veintiuna, I did not know, I did not care to know. This witless man had thought to try cheating on a madwoman with a sword.

Perhaps he decided her sword was just decoration. More fool he. On the road we traveled, only swordsmen carried steel; otherwise the blade will be prized away and the owner's life along with it.

Donna Quick made short work of such challengers. I never needed to carry a sword.

Miguel squeezed my hand a bit more roughly than necessary. I pulled away from his amorous grasp. This was not the time to continue with courting; I shook my head while smiling slightly to indicate not now but absolutely later.

He waggled his eyebrows at me and jerked his chin. Either he had come down with some nervous disease or he was trying to convey a message. I had never been good at semaphore; I eased closer to him and whispered, "Not now!"

"Do something, you idiot!" he whispered back.

He misplaced his confidence in my

abilities. The creaky magic lock on this place prevented use of magic inside the walls. I knew the lock worked, I tried it automatically when I first walked in and received a bit of a shock for my trouble. An old habit, this trying of locks.

I could not magic inside, but perhaps I could create a distraction outside the doors. I could not shove the doors open, but I could pull them from outside; it was a bit of a trick, involving visualization and concentrated throwing of the fields of power, but within my talents.

The doors splashed open with thuds of wood smacking wood, enough to distract Donna from her cutwork. A passing cart and horse transformed into a slow-moving fire-streaming dragon; impressive if I do say so myself. Screams from the crowd gathered outside the tavern, from people walking the streets, from the driver of the sudden dragon himself.

Someone outside shouted, "Beware, a dragon!"

Bingo.

Donna Quick swung her booted foot high and strong into the thigh muscle of the cheater on the floor. His whining pleas for help transformed into screams of agony. I taught her that move. Before she met me, she had been too fine a person to ever consider kicking a downed opponent. Slice him like bologna, yes, but kick? That was my

kind of trick, designed to keep an opponent down while I made a quick getaway.

Donna charged through the tavern doors. She shouted something about waiting, about death to dragons, about how she would rescue any who needed rescue; her usual battlefield declarations.

Once they could breathe again, the men and women of the tavern talked in excited voices, rehashing the events, retelling the story, getting the details settled. More than one person sidled up to the cheater on the floor and kicked him again. He was not going anywhere.

Miguel offered me another drink, a neat shot of amber whiskey, and it broke my heart to turn him down but I needed to find Donna Quick and get us back on the road before the cheater and his friends developed a desire for revenge.

I shrugged and smiled at Miguel, then snagged the cheater's hard leather bag of coin off the floor. I bowed and made my exit.

She was easy to track: people fleeing, dust roiling, yelps of surprise. She was at the end of the street, sitting on the boardwalk, dangling her legs into the street. No one approached her, not even the omnipresent street urchins who stood a respectful distance away from her, watching her every move.

This may in part have resulted from

the ferric cat that climbed into her lap, purring and begging for attention. No one sane wished to handle ferric cats but so very little stopped Donna Quick.

Ferric cats. I glared down at the rust-ball. The damnable things were some meddling iron-monger's brilliant answer to the rodent problem: a mechanical mouser that needed neither care nor concern once loosed on the streets. They bred as rapidly as flesh and blood cats but they did not die as readily. Rust streaks decorated them. They were known to gang up on hapless children and beg for dishes of lubricant oil. Few people were willing to run afoul of these creatures and risk tetanus-laden bites and scratches.

Ferric cats were best left to themselves.

The cat observed my glares and slunk away, leaving speckles of rust on Donna's breeches. She smiled up at me.

"I did not engage the dragon, but I did chase it out of town," she reported. "The beast disappeared in a puff of smoke just as it passed the town limits. I know the direction it ran; we might yet be able to track it to its lair. Perhaps there we can find enough dragon's treasure to make our sojourn to this village worthwhile." She pursed her lips. "I fear I did lose our entire wallet at the gaming table."

As always, I spoke before I thought. "Never fear, mistress. I snagged that cheater's bag of coin before I followed you." I shook the hard leather sack at her, enjoying the metallic jangle of coins rubbing against coins.

Donna Quick frowned. And stood in one graceful movement. And grabbed her sword. Her eyes blazed deep intense green hotter than a farrier's flame.

"You promised that you would never steal again!" She did not quite point her sword at me. "You will return that to its rightful possessor. You are not a thief, Jane. We are not thieves and that is not the name we wish to bear into our futures."

I was not sure if she meant us 'we' or was using a royal 'we,' but the result was the same. I would have to return the coins.

"You are a hard mistress," I whined.

We walked back to our mounts, waiting where we'd left them near the tavern doors. A chubby boy stood beside Donna's mount, not daring to lean on it. When he saw us he swept off his flat cap and sketched an untrained bow.

"If the gentle ladies would please join us inside, we need a word," he said, twisting his face into all kinds of odd shapes as he struggled to remember the message. "I um we, that is, the men of this village, would appre... enjoy... ." He gave up the struggle. "Please ma'ams?"

Donna turned ferocious eyes my way.

"As I said, they believe us thieves and wish to castigate us! You will march in there right now and return that bag of rotted money."

The boy looked at us, unhappy. "I beg your pardon, but both you ma'ams, please, we... they want to see both of you all." He preceded me to the tavern door and held them open. I walked, stiff-backed, certain Donna would prod me with the tip of her sword. She strode along behind me.

The tavern, abuzz until a split-moment before, fell silent like all the good villagers had gone dumb at the same second. The cheater, a bit bruised and bloody, sat in an empty corner and nursed his wounds while glowering at us.

"They will never... " he began but was hissed down by a cascade of sibilant shushes. He glowered yet more.

My mistress showed her teeth and waved her non-sword arm in a regal flutter. "Gentlemen, we have returned to bring to you a favor captured in the heat of battle which rightly belongs not to us but to our worthy opponent." She indicated me and I pulled the bag of coin from my pocket with a good deal of reluctance. "Boy," she said, "fetch this to its owner."

The boy took the bag from my hands and trotted over to the cheater. That man stopped complaining and now looked ready to have a heart attack: red of face, bulging of eye, hard of breath.

Miguel, my gentleman friend from the bar, approached us with two schooners of dark beer in his hands; newly-drawn, by the foaming heads. I unburdened him of one and he offered the other to my mistress.

"Dear ladies, we would like to offer you employment," he said.

The men of the tavern told of the great dragon that afflicted this part of the world, and especially this village. It ate the children, someone said. One morning a week it strode by, the most arrogant worm in creation. The dragon was protected by armed guardsmen, they said, evil men tempted by the dragon's treasure. Would she be willing to help control the beast? Would she, a woman alone, great swordswoman regardless, be able to withstand it and its retinue? Would she, in short, slay the dragon for them?

I rolled my eyes at their story. She was mad, true, but not stupid. Whatever their motivation, she would not be taken in. Though she'd undoubtedly play with them for some time. She had a head for strategy and ambuscade and these men had maps.

I spared little time for their machinations and instead resumed my flirtation with Miguel. He started by holding my hand again, so gently, and before too much longer our lips were pressed against each other and my hands were finding his nether skin very pleasing indeed.

Donna ignored us, stalking up and down the floor like a captured tigress ready to pull apart the bars of her cage. I in turn ignored her. When Miguel whispered against my neck that he had a room upstairs, I let him lead me there.

When I awoke, morning sunlight rounded into the south facing window. The man was not in the room; I could tell from the warmth of the sheets and the scent of him that he left but recently. Perhaps his leaving woke me.

The bed leaned alarmingly and were I prone to hangovers I might have spilt my dinner on the floor. We had broken the bed's farther legs. I giggled at the memory.

Time to pull on my leathers. I pushed aside the curtain and looked down on the town, which did look nicer now than it had the previous day. I saw my black mount below, patiently awaiting me, but not Rosinante. Not Donna's mount.

Ah damnation. I slid into my boots and slammed through the door, startling Miguel returning with his hands full of coffee and food. I pushed by him, stuttered down the stairs, and ran out the twin doors of the tavern.

My mount was covered with a rime of morning dew and street dust. Her mount was indeed gone. I knelt to check the tire marks. She left but recently, and she left in the direction of the dragon's lair.

I hopped on my mount and throttled the engine to life. Miguel was at the doors, then at the rails, still only half-dressed. He shouted something to me. I turned off the engine.

"Tell me fast," I said.

"The train," he said. "The weekly payroll train goes by, guarded by horsemen and never slow enough for us to do anything except stare at it and dream. Donna agreed to help! She'll stop the train long enough for us to get the gold," he said.

"You lied to her, she would never agree to that," I said. "Where is this train, and when is it due?"

"East of town, and north," he said. "It will pass by some time today. The schedule varies. It is protected by a troop of guardsmen who ride alongside and they... they ravage our village on the way through," he said. "We've lost so much. So many. The train doesn't eat our children, those guardsmen do."

"You might have told her that and she would have protected you," I said.

"Think of it: enough gold for all of us to live wealthy for the rest of our lives! Think of it! We can go elsewhere, buy a house, a sturdy bed...." His eyes glazed over with the lust for things which could be bought.

I shook my head. "You mistake us, sir. We are not thieves." I throttled up the engine again and skidded away.

I found her some few miles out of town, her two feet planted on the trestle board between the rails. A swarm of the train's guardsmen milled around her, busy being felled by her sword. A handful of tavern men stood behind her, but most had taken to their heels at the sight of the guardsmen.

Donna faced down the dragon. The train. The enormous black iron steam engine puffing smoke and making hellacious screaming announcements of its closeness. She intended to fight the beast, the worm, the eater of children, and she would be crushed by the locomotive like a snail beneath my boot.

My magic never worked on Donna. I had thought that perhaps the iron of her sword drained it off, but she did not always have the sword at hand. I had thought her madness protected her somehow, charmed safe from the sorcery of cruel or kind hands alike; but I had been able to sorcel other maniacs. Sometimes I believed that her imperviousness to my magic was what kept me at her side.

Perhaps so, but at moments like this, I cursed the woman's slipperiness. Magicking her might be the first and easiest solution, but I could not even throw a protection bubble around her.

I must needs magic the train. Excuse me, the dragon. But the locomotive was made of iron and iron was impervious to magical talents.

If I were a good magician, I would find a way to make the people inside the train safe, or a way to move Donna Quick to safety even though it cost her her blade. If I were a great magician, I would make the locomotive; no: the entire train just up and disappear in a twinkle of sparks.

But I am Jane Smith. I am a magnificent magician.

My feet spread for balance, my arms raised high, I faced the oncoming machine and sorcelled the very atmosphere surrounding the locomotive and its entire train and even the red caboose and all the people and contents. The air solidified and encapsulated the train and then rose up, up into the air, high above the remaining tavern men and the defeated guardsmen and my own beloved Donna Quick. She screamed something about watching the treacherous dragon fly away, but I heard her words through a fog of dimness. The concentration required for this trick was awful and tore at me. I must needs find a safe place to settle said train before my strength gave way.

I decided to encircle the village with the black tail of this dog. A mile of train would do the job nicely.

Donna was mightily frustrated with losing her choice opponent. She revisited her fallen foes, the guardsmen, and set about relieving them of arms and badges. She was more than equal to the task of putting down the ones with enough remaining energy to offer resistance.

Normal times I would have joined her and perhaps taught her new defensive moves against the prone bodies; but I had another debt to settle. What to do? I wracked my brain for a suitable solution to the problem of a tavern filled with men who felt they could use random passersby in their schemes. A lessoning was needed and I was up to teaching it.

I rode my mount back into the village, slow enough to examine the hidden alleys behind the storefronts and the new-created alleys between the train cars. I saw what I needed.

Once again, I could not cast a spell on an iron thing, but there are more ways to skin a cat than the direct route. Fish and lubricant oil, conjured puddles and bowls of the stuff, made a trail to the door of the tavern. The village's army of ferric cats wasted no time in crowding forward, caught by the scent and the promise of oil. Once a goodly number of the rust-balls trotted through the open tavern doors, it took but a wave of my hand to close the doors, another flick of my wrist to lock them in. Shutting the windows and being certain of my thoroughness took but another minute.

I head many satisfying shouts and one or two falsetto screams as the ferric cats made their demands known to the tavern men. Had I an ounce of energy left, I might have smiled.

I did look up at Miguel's window. The curtain was drawn but I saw a shadow-mime played out that convinced me Miguel would never forget this day.

I put the town behind me, my mount roaring steadily, a comfort better than anyone's arms. Donna Quick was easy to spot. She straddled the train tracks, a stack of weaponry piled high beside her, a mass of badges under her feet. I sat next to her. She did not acknowledge me but stared down into a puddle of water formed in gravel at the tracks.

She looked long at her reflection. Her true reflection.

"Jane, fetch me my mirror!" she cried at last.

But me, I was all magicked out. I shook my head. My weariness was such that shaking my head was an effort. I stared down at my dusty boots.

The expected thunderstorm did not break over my poor head. Instead she sat next to me in the dirt, carefully stretched her arm around my shoulder, and let me rest my head against her breast.

"You must think me a great fool, to not notice," she said. "I see your broken heart and my own aches for you, sweet Jane. Yet what would you have me do: pine along with you, face ravaged by sadness, for the dreams and men forever out of our grasp? I think not. I think we must continue our quest. The one true thing is out there, and it is up to us to find it."

Her embrace tightened into a hug; a hug from Donna Quick, would wonders never cease? She stood and wiped dirt from her leather britches and approached her mount, Rosinante, without a backward glance at me.

I stared after her. The quest. Yes, it was all about the quest. How could this madwoman be so right?

Perhaps this was why I followed her. Among all the myriad reasons.

I dragged myself upright and clambered onto my own gentle mount. Her motor thrum was all but drowned out by Rosinante's roar. Donna shouted over the noise.

"Hurry, Jane. Whilst fighting those guardsmen I did spy some giants on that yonder hillside, flailing their arms and threatening to march on the nearest hapless village."

"You mean the windmills? That's the town's windmill farm, their electrical supply..."

"The giants, Jane. I must slay them."

I was engulfed in a plume of road dust as Donna Quick kicked Rosinante into overdrive.

I grinned and followed her, my personal grail, into our glorious madness.

———————————————————

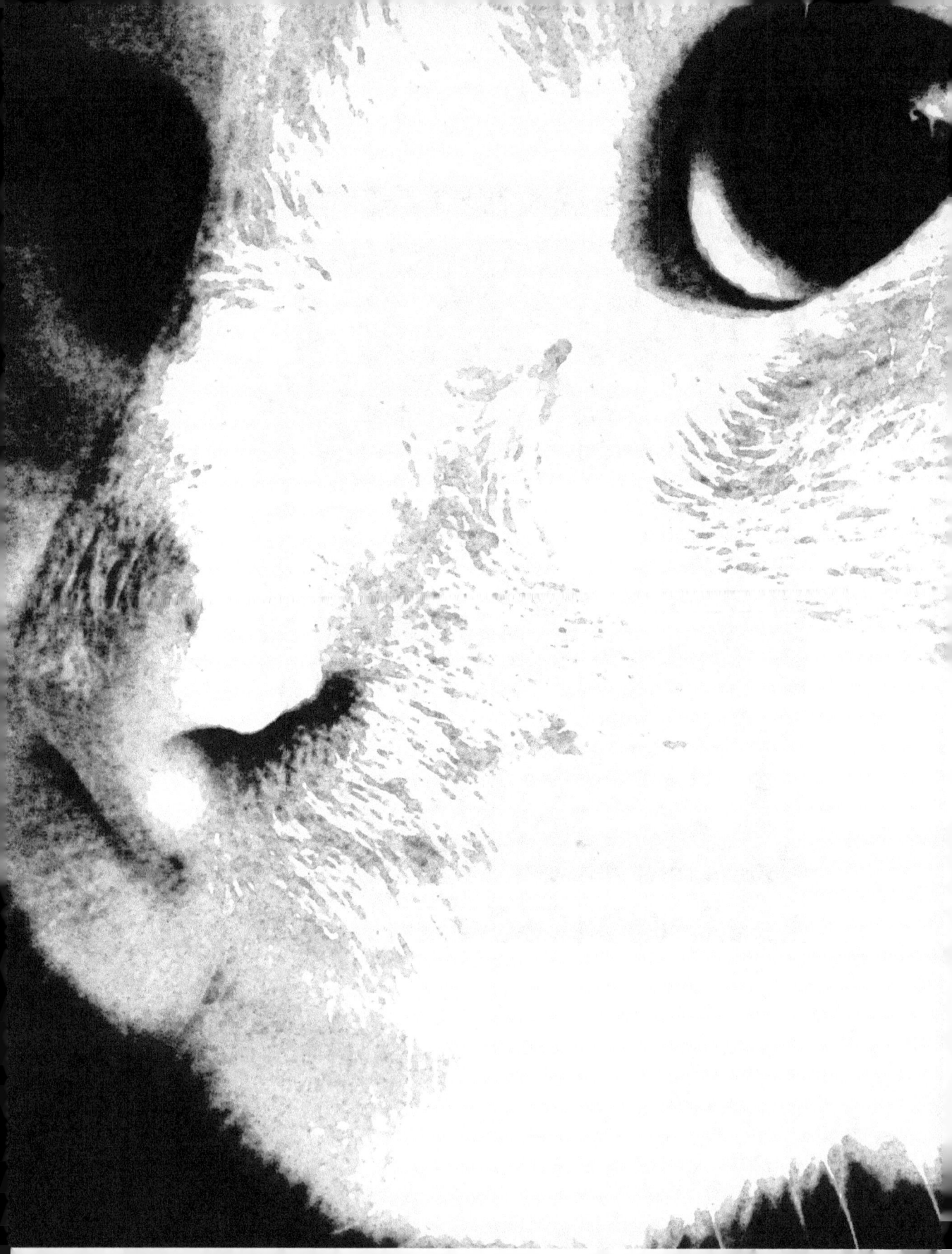

Dividing Lines

by
Lawrence Conquest

Herein, parting and hoping and holding tight

"So, you're really going through with it, then?" My words sounded hollow. I already knew it was a lost cause, but I felt obligated to put up at least a token resistance. Our relationship must have been worth that much.

"David, we've already been through this a hundred times," sighed Sheila. "And we both agreed it was for the best. There's no going back."

I didn't bother to reply. She was right of course. Eventually you have to hold your hands up and admit defeat. Our relationship was over. We'd tried patching it up so many times before, but this time the life had finally gone out of it. There simply wasn't any point in going through the charade again. We'd only end up back at this point. Better to get it over with here and now.

"My car's outside," Sheila continued. "The sooner I get my stuff and go, the better."

I tried adopting a conciliatory tone. "How is your new flat anyway?"

"Fine, David. Just fine. It just feels a little bare at the moment. A little impersonal, you know?"

"Sure," I replied. "Mind you, at least now you'll be away from all my junk."

I smiled to show that I was only joking, but we both knew the truth. I was a reader, a collector, a typical male hoarder. I just don't like throwing things out, especially books. So what if I'd probably never read them again? They were my possessions and I liked having them around. Just knowing they were there was comforting.

Unfortunately Sheila was the opposite. She liked open, airy spaces. A few well-placed ornaments and family photographs, but absolutely no clutter. She said she felt hemmed in by all my books, as if they were looming over her all the time. Go figure.

But some people still believe that everybody's perfect partner is out there, somewhere. Someone who will complement your life and personality to the fullest degree. Your opposite half ~

98

Anyway, it wasn't the deal breaker, it wasn't the deciding factor in why we split up. It was nothing we couldn't have worked around, if we'd wanted to. It was just one of two dozen little things that all added up to two people who simply shouldn't live together.

I watched Sheila as she moved about the house, placing her few remaining possessions into a large black bin liner. I realised this would probably be the last time for her between these four walls and tried to fix the image of her in my mind. Some people believe that buildings can absorb the essences of those who have lived within them. I wondered if I would be haunted by the ghost of Shelia in the weeks and months to come, if I would feel a phantasmal echo of her presence, only to look up and find her gone. Haunted by the ghost of someone who hadn't even died. That about summed me up.

"I think that's it," she said eventually, dragging the by now bulging black sack back to the front door.

"Here – let me." I hoisted the bag aloft, my last chivalrous act for my one-time girlfriend, and carried it outside. The back seat of her car was already crammed tight with cardboard boxes. I could remember moving those same boxes into our house a year before and the giddy sense of excitement I had felt at the time. The future had seemed so full of promise back then, but it had all

come to nothing. I turned away before I could let it affect me further. I had to be practical right now. I had to see this thing through. Time enough for emotions later.

"Well – that's that." Sheila hesitantly walked towards me and we shared an awkward final embrace. Eventually she broke away and turned back towards her car. She opened the driver's side door but before she could get in she let out a strangled yelp and stood up hurriedly. She had seen something ambling down the pavement towards her. Something, or rather someone that she knew.

"Chester!" she cried. "Oh my God, I nearly forgot the cat! What was I thinking of?"

Sheila slammed the car door shut and raced to meet Chester. The cat let out a chirruping meow of greeting and arched his back up towards the expected stroke. As Sheila knelt down to pet him he rubbed himself against her legs, purring like a well-oiled engine.

I was shocked. "Chester? You can't take Chester. He's my cat!"

"I think you'll find he belongs to me, actually," Sheila replied. "You do remember giving him to me as a Christmas present, don't you?"

"Well – yes. But still. He's my cat. And besides, you won't have room for him in your flat, surely?"

"Oh come off it, David. You know as well as I do that Chester spends every possible moment outside. He only comes in for food and sleep."

That much was true. Chester was a pedigree cat, a brown spotted Bengal. As a kitten, we had at first intended to restrict his movements to the house, but he had terrorized us so thoroughly that eventually we gave in and started letting him out. As soon as we did so he became an entirely new character. No longer did he wake us up in the middle of the night, howling like a deranged hyena. No longer did he launch unprovoked attacks on both us and the furniture with seemingly unretractable claws. Instead he expended his energy outside and showed his appreciation by transforming into a loving and lovable pet.

"Well I can't give him up!" I cried. "I simply refuse to do it."

Sheila paused in her stoking. Chester was now lying on his back, his orange and brown spotted belly exposed for the world to see. Sheila slowly ran one fingernail from his neck down to his lower abdomen. Chester mewled in delight. "Well, I suppose there is one other option," she said.

"Oh – and what's that?"

"We could always share him."

Three months later I found myself sitting in my back garden and feeling positive for a change. Sheila had arrived on one of her weekly visits and sat beside me, basking in the summer heat. It was my day off, the sun was out and I had a cold beer in my hand. All of a sudden life seemed bearable. I realised I was grinning and found it difficult to stop.

"Look at him. He's loving it, isn't he?" Sheila pointed towards Chester, who was racing about the garden as though possessed. He suddenly arced his back and flipped himself into the air, his mouth snapping shut on an innocent cabbage moth that had made the mistake of fluttering nearby. Poor bastard.

"Yeah, he certainly loves his playing," I agreed. "It's nice to see him running about like this. I don't suppose he's able to do much of that at yours?"

Sheila looked pensive. "Well, it's true he hasn't really gone out much. Not yet, anyway. I think he's still getting used to the situation. He'll be fine though. He's a real lap cat now."

I just bet he is, I thought. Still, there was no denying it was nice to see Chester having so much fun. Luckily - or unluckily depending on how you looked at it – Sheila and I had never got around to having a family of our own. So in many ways Chester was like the son we never had. It was understandable that neither of us wanted to be parted from him.

"Anyway," Sheila continued. "Lovely as all this is, I'm afraid I really do have to be going soon. Marcus is meeting me for lunch."

"Oh, really?" I tried to stay in a positive frame of mind and not to think about her new boyfriend. I shouldn't begrudge her moving on. And who knew – perhaps one day soon I'd find someone new myself?

"Yes. Sorry, I did promise him. Come on. Let's get it over with. Chester!" The cat looked up as Sheila called his name. She clicked her fingers and whistled at him. Chester approached at a hesitant lope, his shoulders slumped, as if well aware that play time was over.

Sheila scooped up the cat in her arms and cooed at it like a baby. "It's alright, kitty kitty. It's OK." She raised an eyebrow at me. "Come on, David, hurry up. Let's not make this difficult on him."

I sighed and stepped closer until Chester was cradled between us. I scratched him gently behind the ears. "Come on, big fella. You've done this before. You know it doesn't hurt."

I nodded at Sheila. It was time. We positioned ourselves around Chester, her holding his right-hand side, me holding his left. Keeping a firm hold, we began to draw apart.

In truth pulling Chester apart took no more effort than peeling open a banana.

The cat split cleanly down the middle, a dividing line opening up from the top of his nose down to the tip of his tail. There was absolutely no blood, no spillage. There never was. As we pulled apart I could see Chester's internal organs exposed to view like an illustrated anatomical cross section. There was his severed heart, still beating rapidly like some fragile, tremulous bird. Upon each side of the widening divide a lung continued to inflate and deflate, their synchronicitous movements turning ragged and mismatched as the cat's two halves slowly gained independence.

In short, it looked as though Chester had run face first through a band-saw.

I turned my half of the bisected cat around to face his opposite half. The mismatched mirror images stared curiously at each other for a moment, before touching half-noses in a hesitant greeting. Before they could start grooming each other I placed my half of Chester upon the ground. He rubbed himself weakly against my legs, both marking me and using me as a ready-made crutch to lean against.

"I'll see you next week then, hopefully," said Sheila, placing her own half of cat into a large carpet bag. The bifurcated animal mewled softly in the darkness, the outline of its body visible as it gently pushed against the material that enclosed it. My half of Chester waddled forwards as best he could and sat down before the bag. I tried not to look as he akwardly reached up with his sole front leg and tentatively pawed at the outline of his hidden half. "If not it will be the week after. Marcus has some time off next week and we might want to go somewhere."

All of a sudden I felt a wave of bitterness sweep over me. The positive feelings I had been basking in earlier had vanished without a trace. It was as though the dividing of Chester had reopened the jagged wounds in our own relationship.

"Fine," I said sarcastically. "Turn up when you feel like it. I'm sure Chester won't mind. You've got your own life to lead after all. You've made that perfectly clear."

Sheila scowled. "Don't you dare try and use Chester as a weapon against me. We both know your own happiness is the only thing you care about. I'm leaving now. You can just stay here and stew in your own misery."

And with that, she was gone.

When people enter into a relationship, they have this notion about two becoming one. It's a romantic thought, noble even - but its bullshit, really. People are individuals. Always have been, always will be. The best you can hope for is someone who'll put up with your idiosyncrasies, somebody who'll let you be what you want to be - at least enough of the time for you to survive. Compromise is the key.

But some people still believe that everybody's perfect partner is out there, somewhere. Someone who will complement your life and personality to the fullest degree. Your opposite half – just waiting to be pressed tight against you until you both become part of a greater whole. Well - perhaps they're right, but it's a big world out there, and I haven't found my other half yet.

Once Sheila had gone I picked up Chester's body and led him back to the garden. I guided him through the air as though he was some kind of furry Spitfire. He bared his teeth at the hovering moths but his heart just wasn't in it. It wasn't fun anymore.

When it began to get dark I carried Chester inside and leant him up against the mantelpiece. He doesn't normally mind. Usually he'll just stand there looking like a stuffed animal - or at least one half of a stuffed animal - with only the watchful motion of his single green eye reminding me that he's actually alive.

But tonight he seemed restless, as though eager for something more. Chester stretched his limbs, and made as if to move across the mantelpiece, across the tacky carriage clock and the framed photograph of Sheila and myself. Back when we were two. Back when we were both joined at the hip.

But he's not ready yet. Chester slipped and nearly fell, but I rushed across the room and held him steady. His balance is all wrong. He still isn't used to the single life.

Maybe one day Chester will learn to stand on his own two feet. Or maybe one day he'll be reunited with his other half, and I with mine.

We live in hope.

Me and Susan Smiling at the Beach

by
Jeremy Schliewe

Herein the potential for chipped teeth... and worse.

Susan called a couple of weeks ago. Just like that--as if ten years of silence had been nothing more than an awkward pause in a long conversation. I recognized her voice immediately--low and smoky. Back in the old days it could quickly change registers and erupt into a bright peal of laughter. I had always been able to make her laugh.

"I have some vacation coming up," she said. She wasted no time, dispensing with our small talk after the how-are-yous. Something told me she wasn't in a laughing mood.

"Mm?" It was the best I could manage.

"I was thinking about flying out to see you."

After Susan had left me, she met someone new and moved to Florida. They married. I don't know whether they had children or not, or even if she was still with the guy. A lot can happen in ten years. Maybe there was trouble at home and she was laying the groundwork for an affair. Maybe she had divorced and was hoping to rekindle our old romance. Maybe, hoping to allay any regrets or perhaps compare me to her husband, she was curious to see what type of person I had grown into. We had always said that no matter what happened we'd remain friends. We hadn't, of course, but any bitterness I had felt had long since died and the memories I had of her and I were, for the most part, happy.

So there we were, after exchanging a handful of sentences over the telephone, falling right back into that silence, adding long seconds to our running tally of ten years. She needed my answer.

"Come out," I said.

"I'll be there on Tuesday. My flight gets in at three."

"You don't have to sleep on the couch." She said it quickly, as if her words were in a race against me to the door. "There's plenty of room in bed."

It wasn't like me to make rash decisions. Susan's visit could potentially turn my life on its ear, or so I told myself. But the truth was, aside from the job I kept at a company specializing in wireless communication, I would not have a great deal of trouble accommodating a guest. I had fallen into a state in which I half-expected to spend the rest of my life, neither terribly happy nor terribly sad. Life had offered me a kind of numb comfort and I took it, perhaps out of fear that a large disturbance in any direction would knock me out of whack and send my boat for choppy waters.

She had rung off before I could get any more information out of her. I didn't want to bombard her with questions--I knew I'd get all the answers I needed when I saw her in person. Maybe I had been in a ten-year rut and needed a mystery.

I dug out from my closet an old shoe box filled with photographs; me and Susan at the Shedd Aquarium; Susan in the kitchen, rolling pizza crust with her hair pulled back, her hands dusted with flour; me and Susan smiling at the beach. She was a pretty girl, with long brown hair--much too pretty for a guy like me. But I had made her laugh. I wondered if she were still pretty. She was still plenty young, but people our age stand at a crossroads in terms of physical attractiveness--we have been presented with ample opportunities to let ourselves go and many among us, especially those lulled by the false sense of security that comes with marriage, relax by slow degrees--until the day we wake up and find ourselves no longer young or attractive.

I didn't expect it would be the case with Susan. Even when a year into our relationship Susan quit smoking she didn't gain an ounce. She had been a regular runner and kept to a reasonably healthy diet. In her early twenties she was radiant, the type that was sure to age gracefully. I had even met her mother and in my mind breathed a relieved sigh--for Susan, it was one possible future I could happily accept.

Again I looked at the photograph of us at the beach, Susan tan and trim in her bikini. She was a generous lover and if she lacked anything in the realm of acrobatics she more than made up for it in enthusiasm. Sometimes she'd even apologize afterwards, as if she had fumbled her way through our coupling and somehow left me less than satisfied. Nothing could have been further from the truth. I held a secret hope that that part of Susan still existed and, if things went well, we'd have occasion to revisit those old times.

Truth be told, Susan's ending our relationship had hurt me more than I ever let on. Some part of me had always longed for her and perhaps always would. Over the past ten years I had mapped in my mind possible realities in which she had not moved away, realities in which we stayed together, moved in, got married, did all of those things that people in love do. I have never been able to give myself fully to a woman since and as a result, the bulk of my time I passed alone. Let her come, I thought. Any change she brings will be welcome.

I drove to the airport and waited at the terminal for Susan to disembark. We hadn't talked since the day she called, so the possibility that she wasn't on the flight was at the forefront of my mind. The door opened and, led by a flight attendant pushing a red wheelbarrow, passengers began to file out of the jet bridge and into the terminal. I stood up, ran a hand through my hair, and searched the weary travelers. With each unfamiliar face that appeared in the corridor, my hope diminished. Had Susan called me out just to stand me up? Maybe, in nervous anticipation that I was not the same Charlie anymore, she had been unable to board the airplane and close the distance between us.

When traffic out of the airplane had stopped, I walked to the open doorway to peer down the jet bridge. A man in a pilot's uniform sauntered toward me and, reading my face like a question, put a hand on my shoulder.

"Sorry, son. There's no one else."

There was nothing to do but go home. So much for Susan, so much for my all my plans. I turned and began to walk away when I heard her voice behind me.

"I was beginning to think you changed your mind."

"I was thinking the exact--" I spun on my heel to track the voice. I faced not Susan, but the red-haired flight attendant, the first to leave the airplane. She smiled a pretty smile at me, but blinked in rapid succession as if trying to fight back some emotion bubbling within. She was an attractive woman to be sure, but not Susan.

"I'm sorry," I said. "I thought you were someone else."

"Down here, silly."

I followed the flight attendant's slender arms down to the wooden handles of the wheelbarrow she clutched in her pale hands--I traced the lacquered arms of the wheelbarrow to the shiny red basin. I was scarcely prepared for what I saw inside. Could this amorphous lump of flesh and hair be the woman I once loved? Completely naked, with only a blanket between her skin and the cold metal, the thing inside conformed to the basin's shape like a dollop of tapioca pudding. I could discern neither arms nor legs and the face seemed anchored by only the most tentative force--there were her blue eyes all right, staring up at me from some willy-nilly place on what I would hesitate to call a body. The brown hair that had once fallen onto her tanned shoulders now floated atop her shapelessness like a slime-slicked curl of seaweed on a pool of stagnant water.

"Susan?"

"Unobservant as ever, I see," the thing in the wheelbarrow chuckled. "It's good to see you, Charlie."

I couldn't get Susan into my coupe. I had to hail a cab--one of those minivans with a removable back seat. Fortunately, she had checked no luggage; the sum of her travel necessities amounted to a blanket and wheelbarrow. Susan said she was hungry--airlines these days were unwilling to part with more than a bag of pretzels and a half-cup of orange juice. She suggested we stop at Pruebelo, a little Mexican restaurant that we had gone to from time to time for tacos and happy hour margaritas. She said it sounded like a great idea.

I took mine on the rocks, she blended--and with a straw so that I could lower the glass to her level and help her drink. The waiter, consummate professional he was, held an unfaltering smile as he pulled a chair away from the table to accommodate the wheelbarrow. Susan seemed happy on the surface, though I had the feeling that something was wrong--why else would she come halfway across the country to see me?

"How's your husband?"

"He's good."

Again came the silence that had become a recurring theme in our relationship. It had not always been that way. When we were together, we always had something to talk about-- even the quiet times carried with them no awkwardness. Maybe it was easier because then we were young and the future seemed far away.

I wanted to ask her what had happened to change her so, but decided to wait, not wanting to seem overly eager to bring up a potentially delicate subject. It seemed to me that Susan had no skeleton, that she had been deboned like a fish. Her arms and legs were gone, or had been stretched to the point of nonexistence by her lack of inner framework. It was not that she had put on weight, rather than her weight had been redistributed with her new shape. Susan looked up at me and smiled. Somehow she was able to keep her facial features oriented. She could face upward and slightly forward, as if she possessed some limited range of motion. I fed her a taco, being careful not to spill meat on her naked body. I wiped her mouth with a paper napkin, took a drink, and held up my glass to order another.

"How long you here?"

"As long as you can stand me. I got an open-ended ticket," she said.

"That must've cost a fortune," I said. I didn't want to offer my opinion on the subject of her departure just yet. "Is there anything special you want to do while you're here?"

"All the old things," she said. "Everything we used to do."

I took my bed apart and leaned the disassembled frame and box spring mattress against the wall. With just the top mattress resting on the floor, I could spill Susan out of the wheelbarrow and into bed. I tipped the wheelbarrow and poured her onto the bed. She rolled out like warm, flesh-colored taffy. I saw a couple of fingernails--maybe toenails, and a little dimple I took to be her navel--the navel I had so long ago probed with my tongue, prompting Susan to pull up her legs and giggle and squirm. A triangular patch of pubic hair slipped over the lip of the wheelbarrow, soon followed by her facial features, which flopped forward onto the mattress. Her muffled cries for help began immediately--she'd suffocate if I didn't do something. I thrust my hands into her doughy body and strained to

lift her, having no more elaborate a plan than to keep shifting her mass until her face was no longer under her body. I have never been terribly strong. I could feel my stomach muscles strain and beginnings of cramps in my forearms. I struggled--it was like trying to gather a gigantic wet blanket in my arms; the more I turned her weight, the less I felt I was making any progress. Finally I heard her voice, clear and loud.

"Charlie! It's okay! You can put me down!"

I dropped her and she landed on the mattress with a phumph. There she was, looking up at me with those blue eyes, breathing hard but smiling.

"My," she said. "You're really red."

"Yeah," I said, gasping. "I imagine I am."

I started to laugh. I don't know why. I didn't find things particularly funny. Rather, I wanted to cry or scream or run away. Susan joined me laughing. Susan, the blob on my bed. For a second our laughter took on a conspiratorial quality, as if she were reading my mind and me hers.

I spent the night on the couch. Susan said that I didn't have to--she didn't want to put me out. But she was a guest and I wanted her to be comfortable. Besides, I had fallen asleep on the couch plenty of times watching television.

110

I got little sleep. The thought of what lie on the other side of the living room wall was not easily shooed from my mind. Through the vent set near the ceiling, I could hear the steady, muffled sound of Susan's voice. I thought at first she had developed the habit of talking in her sleep. I got up from the couch to try and listen in. Perhaps whatever she was saying could shed some light on her situation. But when I neared the register I realized that Susan was not talking. She was crying.

We had a picnic at the park the next day--it wasn't much of a park. During our senior year in college we had frequented it because it was just a short walk from a house I had rented on the east side of town. On a tuft of grass overlooking a reed-rimmed pond we ate sandwiches and pasta salad, a meal I had prepared in the morning while Susan, tired from her flight, slept in.

"This is just what I wanted, Charlie," Susan said. "Thanks."

"Wait," I said. "There's more." I took a towel-wrapped bottle of chilled Chardonnay from the backpack I had worn, along with a couple of plastic wine glasses. I assembled them, attaching the stems and feet to the bowls, and poured two glasses. The sunlight caught the wine and shot the plastic cup full of light and a bright topaz formed inside. A breeze rustled the cattails and rippled the water. I kneeled and brought the glass over the lip of the wheelbarrow. Susan sat up, so that some of her mass was resting on the back of the bucket, as one does against a pillow while reading in bed. Whatever musculature it was that worked inside the shapeless lump of her body had pulled her face up and forward facing, allowing me to tilt the wine glass to her lips without spilling.

"What's this?" she asked.

"Chardonnay," I said.

"I know it's Chardonnay," she said. "But since when do we drink it out of glasses?" She put on a smile and batted her eyelashes. If her facial features could be isolated, Susan would indeed be the same pretty girl I had known-- though that prettiness was now but a vessel adrift on an unchartable sea of repulsiveness. "On picnics we always used drink from the bottle, passing it back and forth. Don't you remember?"

I remembered. Of course I remembered.

"I don't know," I said. "I don't want to chip a tooth."

Having now had some experience in the matter, it was easier getting Susan into bed that night. I threw a thin blanket over most of her, not so much because she was cold, but to give my eyes a break from the frightening tedium that came with the gravity she exuded. What had made her that way? She seemed reluctant to talk about it. The smile she had put on so many times since she arrived seemed to mask a profound sadness. I had always been able to detect Susan's mood shifts, no matter how subtle. Something inside her had changed over the past ten years. She was no longer the bright, athletic girl I had loved. Something had happened in Florida that had robbed her of her cheerfulness. Physical transformation aside, the Susan who lay on my bed was not the same who had ten years ago traded one peninsula for another and left her absence hanging like a fog in my lonely little home.

I stood in the doorway, my hand on the light switch, when Susan spoke.

"He left me," she said. "Steve's gone."

"Steve?" I searched my memory.

"My husband," she said. "My ex-husband."

I had never even known the guy's name. Steve . . . it somehow seemed appropriate. A flame of jealousy leapt through my guts and was gone. I did not know what to say.

"The divorce was final last week. I had to get out of there. That place. It was too . . . Depressing."

With that she started to sob. Tears rolled out of her eyes, over the shallow convexity of her body, and onto the bed. Great, sad convulsions rippled through her. I thought of the night, long ago, when she had gotten a call from her mother that a beloved cat had to be put to sleep. Leaning against the wall, she sat on the kitchen floor and cried, her long legs thrust out in front of her. Her hair fell on her face and I could only see flashes of her dewy eyes and wet red cheeks as she drew a hand across to wipe her tears. Slowly losing the willingness to sit, she slid down the wall until she was lying on the floor. She was radiant, even then. I sat down next to her. We hadn't been together very long and I was unsure how to go about the business of offering comfort. I gave her my hand and she took it damply in hers. Before long, I was lying next to her with my hand on her stomach and my nose, lost in a tangle of hair and tears, itching as its tip brushed her warm cheek. I recall even then the desire such closeness stirred in me, and the niggling sense of guilt that came with wanting someone so vulnerable.

"I'm sorry to hear about the divorce," I said. I left the light on and began taking tentative steps toward the mattress. The lump under the blanket jiggled with its rhythmic gasping. "Look," I continued, not really knowing what I was going to say. "You're on vacation now. You don't have to think about it--about any of it. You're here

112

now and let's just make the most of it."

She kept crying. I tried again. "We can do anything you want while you're here. You're in my hands now. Think of me as your personal assistant."

It seemed to help. Susan's crying had quieted and after a couple of soft sniffles she offered a feeble "Okay."

"That's better," I said. "I'm going to turn out the light now."

"You don't have to sleep on the couch." She said it quickly, as if her words were in a race against me to the door. "There's plenty of room in bed."

"You're tired," I said. "You need some rest. I tend to toss and turn. You'd be better off without me."

My sleep was fitful. Each time I awoke, I could hear Susan's steady sobbing through the vent in the wall that separated the living room from the bedroom. The happy face she put on during the day seemed so easily cast aside at night. I thought of that other bit of information Susan had neglected to share with me: How much longer was she planning to stay?

We spent the next day at the zoo--Susan seemed somewhat cheered by the animals--and in the evening took an early dinner at an Italian restaurant.

"I'm sorry if I'm a lot to put up with," she said.

"Not at all. It's nice having you here. It's no disruption at all, really."

"You're not seeing anyone?"

"Me? No . . . "

"It's hard to believe. You were always so sweet. I can't believe no one's come along and scooped you up."

"I've dodged a few bullets," I lied. Susan flashed a brief smile at this, as if it somehow confirmed to her idea of the Charlie she had left in Michigan.

"You're sure I'm not a bother? I feel like you're always having to tend to me."

"It's no worse than the time you quit smoking," I said. "That was a bother. In fact, I sometimes think it's the real reason we broke up."

"Oh," she said and cast her in another direction. "Steve never did like my smoking."

"Steve?"

"I've got a confession, Charlie."

We stopped eating and Susan told me about Steve. She had met him while we were still together and they started seeing each other on the sly. It prompted her to quit smoking. I had never smoked, but Susan's habit never bothered me--I had always thought her quitting was more of a strain than the habit itself. Steve, apparently, saw it differently. Susan had always told me it was something she was doing for herself. The serene days we had passed together became punctuated by flashes of white-hot argument--instances I had chalked up to Susan going through nicotine withdrawal. Before long, we were over and I had no idea the real reason why until now.

"I'm sorry, Charlie," she said. She had tears in her eyes.

"It was all so long ago. Water under the bridge, right?"

"I've always regretted it. Even when I was happy with Steve. It was unfair to you. And now look where it's got me."

"We don't have to talk about this," I said. "It's ancient history. Who cares? Let's eat." I stabbed my fork into my spaghetti noodles and twirled them.

She smiled. Either my lack of a strong reaction or the act of confession had given her some relief.

"I'm not hungry anymore," she said. "Look at us. All we do is eat."

"That's what people do."

"Why haven't you taken me to the beach?" she asked.

I parked the van I had rented for Susan's stay at the State Park and wheeled her down the ramp. I knew it would be folly to push Susan's wheelbarrow across the sand, so we opted for a walk to the end of the pier. The sunsets, with only the wavy expanse of Lake Michigan to contrast with the sky, are some of the most beautiful I have ever seen. Gray swaths of woolly clouds stretched themselves at lazy angles to the horizon and the sky was already showing sherbet colors of pink and orange. The red lighthouse stood sentry at the end of the structure, sweeping the sky with its silvery eye.

Ignoring the warning signs--"This Structure Is Not Designed for Public Access: Walk At Your Own Risk"--and passing the stone memorial dedicated to the lives of those lost on the pier, I wheeled Susan along. The wheel bumped over the ruts in the concrete and I had to steer in and out of the iron struts of the catwalk in order to negotiate a clear path. There were surprisingly few people out for such a mild evening. Susan, like a child in a stroller, had the luxury of watching the world unfold before her. She took in the scene with a gloss-eyed wonder.

"Oh, this is lovely, Charlie."

A couple of old fisherman dangled their legs over the edge and sat patiently with their poles poised in the air, hoping to land a straggler from the late summer salmon run. A pair of teenage girls giggled into their fingers when they saw us pass. A couple holding hands made a show of looking the other direction and I felt lonelier than ever.

I maneuvered Susan past the lighthouse and we found ourselves on the platform with nothing between us and the horizon but a field of copper-green water. I looked down at her. She seemed happier, as if her confession had cleared her conscience. But what was the point? I certainly didn't feel any better. In fact, I felt like an old wound had been re-opened. When Susan and I ended I was heartbroken. Now there was another layer on top of it--I had been deceived. She had brought it on herself, whatever it was that had transformed her into this hideous thing. She deserved her sadness, her jellyfish body. No wonder Steve had left her--how could you blame him? But I was jumping to conclusions; I did not know when Susan's transformation took place. It very well could have happened after Steve left.

As Susan admired the changing sky, I looked at the waters that lapped the lip of the pier. I could push her and the wheelbarrow right off the edge and be done with it. Who would miss her? I looked around and saw nobody nearby, except for the fishermen halfway down the length of the pier, intent on their bobbers. I grabbed the wooden handles of the wheelbarrow and moved toward the edge.

"Charlie, what are you doing?"

I kept walking.

"Christ, Charlie, be careful. Don't forget I can't swim."

"Oh. Sorry." I stopped pushing the wheelbarrow, its single tire at the edge of the concrete. I didn't have it in me. I wasn't cut out for murder. I pointed at the water. "Sometimes you can see fish swimming along those rocks."

We spent the next two days inside. The sadness Susan had brought with her began to take a hold of me. On the second night Susan confessed that she had regretted leaving me for Steve. It was the greatest mistake of her life, she said, and that she had come back to salvage whatever vestige of our relationship she could. I too had made a mistake. I opened the door to the past and let Susan through. I felt like my insides were slowly turning to mush.

I put her in my bed and steeled myself to ask a question I had been afraid to ask.

"Are you planning on going home anytime soon?"

"No, Charlie. I'm not."

I had somehow suspected it. "You mean you're not going back to Florida?"

"Florida doesn't exist anymore."

Doesn't exist? Was she speaking some sort of riddle? "You mean it doesn't exist for you anymore."

"It doesn't exist at all, Charlie, because I said it doesn't."

"I don't believe you," I said, tightening my chest as I spoke to try and disguise a shaky voice.

"Check a map," she said.

I took the atlas from my bookshelf

and looked at a map of the United States. Sure enough, Florida was gone. The Southeastern corner of the country met the ocean smoothly with the rounded coastlines of Alabama and Georgia.

"I'll be damned," I said. I was completely under her power. I could no longer see things for what they were.

"Now are you coming to bed or what?"

I hesitated. "I guess I am."

I lifted up the covers. Susan was waiting, naked and formless. I climbed in.

"Come to me, my darling."

I did. I lay on my side and put a hand on her yielding flesh, knowing that she'd never leave, that she'd never allow Florida to come back. The ten years we had spent apart was our silent pact of sorrow. It was too late to try and pretend that things could be like they had been. But we were together again nevertheless. I kissed her on the lips. Somewhere deep inside my body I felt something go slack, as if some air I had for too long held in my lungs had escaped and left me deflated.

———————————————

What begins as a routine missing person case for Seattle private eye Dick Hunter turns into a personal vendetta. In this zany adventure, Dick Hunter and the beautiful, angelic Amie team up with a host of magical animal familiars to defeat Mort des Hommes, a hell spawn, before his wicked plans come to fruition. A wickedly funny new book from A. Jarrell Hayes.

"If you enjoy fantasy fiction, *Detecting Magic with Dick Hunter* is worth reading. The plot is interesting, the characters are exciting and humorous, and the story takes place in our own time."

-- Book Reviews Weekly
www.bookreviewsweekly.com

Price: $9.99
ISBN: 978-145-656605-0

Available on Amazon.com and bookstores nationwide.

117

Stone Telling
A Review of Issues 1&2
By Alexandra Seidel

Stone Telling 1: Silence to Speech

Silence to Speech is the title of the first issue of Stone Telling, an online poetry magazine that premiered in 2010. Silence to Speech indeed--rarely has there been a magazine that felt so much like it was giving a voice to those unheard.

Each and every poem in this issue explores speech and explores silence, but most importantly, together they give the reader a feel for what the journey from one to the other means.

The issue opens with Ursula K. Le Guin's *The Elders at the Falls.* This poem speaks of the degeneration of speech and communication--community--into aching silence, leaving the reader raw and suddenly sensitive to what speech means in our lives.

This is perhaps most vividly expressed in Peer Dudda's *Train Go Sorry*, a bilingual poem in English and ASL. Narrated by the poet himself, we are allowed to partake in his journey from one language to the other, from a sense of home shattered to a sense of finding a home in words that need not be said out loud.

J. C. Runolfson in her poem *Robert Cornelius speaks a dead tongue* explores the artist's language, the language of photography in it's early stage. "This is alchemy,/the transmutation of metal into/the image of man,/the capture of this light/in this place,/but it is only the first stage, dissolute." she writes aptly, telling us of a communication that uses images freed from their time, giving a voice to that moment in time even once it has passed.

The poetry section closes with Shweta Narayan's lush bilingual poem *Nagapadam* in which speech and language suddenly appear split tongued, where words may be spoken but are not heard, not understood by the listener.

Concluding the issue is a non-fiction section that shall not be reviewed here, but it is worth a read all the same.

The striking thing about Stone Telling is that all the poems work on so many levels, especially seen as a whole. Out of the fourteen poems eight are accompanied with an audio/video version, allowing the authors to give voice to their own poems, something that adds even more depth to the experience of these works, unbinds them from just being words on paper and transforms them into a tale told in the distinct voices of their creators. The artwork that accompanies most of the poems is tastefully chosen and serves well to tickle the reader's imagination beyond the reading or listening.

Stone Telling 2: The Generation Issue

Stone Telling's second issue is titled *The Generation Issue*, yet it is not apart from what came before, it continues, offers dialogue and further exploration. "If love and bread are made and made again, then voice is found and stifled – here, and gone; is heard, or is dismissed. Always, always it is emerging. It is a work in progress, a word in progress, a silence dormant waiting for the right breath." Lemberg says in the issue's introduction. The theme of generations in this issue often focuses on women, their place in a line of many generations before or after, or their breaking free, their becoming, their choices and losses. The poetry in this issue is not an easy read, it is full of pain and hurt and longing, but the reader is left richer for the experience.

In *Archaeology* by Eliza Victoria, we see a generation broken, a mother who has lost her son and is stuck in her grief,

119

not able to let go of her lost child.

Samantha Henderson tells a family's history as measured by a piece of jewelry in *The Necklace*, where the precious thing itself is broken up to afford a living in a time of strife. In the poem the necklace thus becomes more than just a precious heirloom, it is scattered through history and time, pieces that cannot become whole again, but still are there in the lives the necklace helped support.

The poetry section of the issue ends with Catherynne Valente's *Eight Legs of Grandmother Spider* in which the sun is fetched and one generation goes, leaving behind a grandchild that remembers enough of her grandmother to allow for sadness.

The poets' visions of their works can be heard in many cases--audio files are frequently provided alongside the poems.

The art is delicately picked and feels succinct in the way it complements the poem it is placed with.

Again a rich non-fiction section (that was not reviewed) completes this issue.

It should be mentioned that among the poetry selected for the first two issues of Stone Telling, five poems are nominated for the 2011 Rhysling Award, a prize awarded annually by the SFPA (Science Fiction Poetry Association).

In terms of genre, Stone Telling offers an eclectic mix; there are literary voices alongside those of speculative poems, bilingual poems, prose poems and visual poems and interestingly enough, the editor makes this work without one piece smothering the other.

A visit to the site is highly recommended: ***www.stonetelling.com***

Alexa Chats... with Rose Lemberg

By Alexandra Seidel

Some of our readers may not know who you are. Tell us a bit about yourself.

I'm Rose Lemberg. I was born on the outskirts of the former Hapsburg empire, emigrated to Israel when I was fourteen, came to the US for graduate school, and hopefully am here to stay. I am a native-level speaker of three languages (actually this should be five, but the other two languages are not in as good a shape due to lack of practice). I'm a sociolinguist and work as a professor at a large research university in the Midwest. I'm queer, a mom, a poet, and a writer, in no particular order. I have a yellow thumb, love art glass, cannot sing, and believe that hope is a thing with feathers.

When did you begin to think of yourself as a poet?

Very recently. I've been writing poetry since childhood. I remember writing a long astronomical ode at age eight. It was in Russian. However, the title "poet" is reserved in Russian for the likes of Pushkin and Akhmatova, so I had a real problem with that word as applied to myself. For American speakers of English this works differently; you can self-identify as a poet without having published anything at all. In my case, I think I started cautiously using "poet" to self-identify after *Godfather Death* received a Rhysling nomination (this was my second nomination).

Poetry vs. fiction--one or the other: why do you write poetry and what can a poem do that a story can't?

Poetry is native to me. I love reading it, I studied quite a few languages in order to read poetry in the original, I think about it, and I write it. I love writing fiction too, but I keep returning to poetry again and again, not because it is somehow superior or inferior, but simply because that's where my heart's home is. As for why I'm writing it: in 2008, when I realized that I can actually write a poem in English and sell it, I became more serious about writing my poems down, then saving them, revising them, and sending them out. I compose poetry because I cannot live without it, but I write poetry because people seem to want to read it (and buy it). I have very few things saved from before 2008.

Poetry is great for my fiction too, since it makes me unafraid to use lyrical and unusual imagery in my prose.

Your poems have a very distinct imagery. Salt and masks and birds...tell us a bit about what the images you use mean (to you).

I do write about birds a lot! Perhaps I have birditis. I think each of us in the speculative poetry field has favorite and distinct imagery. Many wonderful speculative poets love the sea. I am not a big fan of the sea. My element is fire: mighty or dying down to nothing, domestic or dangerous, life-giving and yet requiring constant maintenance to continue. Birds, too, embody a dichotomy – that of fragility and flight. I just love birds so much. Naturally, firebirds are the best. My firebird poem *Burns at Both Ends* was nominated for the Dwarf Stars award, and yet another firebird poem *Love's Ecology* is at Apex, for your interest. Recently, I decided to unabashedly embrace my love of birds and bird imagery: I'm writing a YA novel set in Birdverse, a secondary world with a Bird deity. The Goddess Bird is a polybird: she can appear as many different birds, depending on the believer's culture and character. I am rather foolishly fond of all this.

Also, formatting is something you work with a lot. What is the idea/concept behind that?

I work less with formatting now that I know how hard it is to digitize poetry with a lot of formatting! When it does happen, it's sort of intuitive – some poems are just kinetic, they want to move and breathe. *Reap the Whirlwind* in Jabberwocky 5 is like that – appropriately, it's a poem about winds.

Is there any one achievement in your writing career that stands out? What is it and why is it so special?

Hm. There are two, actually. One is my Jewish fantasy short story *Geddarien*, which came out in Fantasy Magazine in December 2008. It is a story about two klezmer musicians, a grandfather and grandson, during the Holocaust. This story received a lot of attention: honorable mentions from Rich Horton and Gardner Dozois, and a reprint in *People of the Book: a Decade of Jewish Science Fiction and Fantasy*, where it appears alongside work by Michael Chabon, Neil Gaiman, and Jane Yolen. I have a few Jewish-themed works in the pipeline; my current favorite is probably my April 2011 Apex poem, *Thirteen Principles of Faith.*

My second accomplishment is not an accomplishment yet. It is something I call "ten days in December." In December 2010, I was struck by an immense wave of inspiration; over the span of ten days I wrote an epic poem in six parts, and a novelette (1300 and 13000 words respectively); both pieces are set in secondary worlds, and are LGBTQ-themed; both are now on submission. I felt so much better about my writing after this happened, that I wrote a lot of new prose pieces, and am now working on a novel.

Why do you write? And is there some sort of underlying theme that connects all your works?

I write fiction because of an event that happened to me in the summer of 2007, that enabled me to start writing out of my worlds. I write about marginal identities, cultures in contact and in conflict, loss, love, languages, generations, silence and speech - the themes that are also reflected in the kind of work I select for Stone Telling. Nothing straightforward. I guess I write about what it means to be me; but we're all doing that.

The understanding and enjoyment of poetry is culture specific. What do you think?

Sure, just as our language shapes the way we think. But what happens if you're multilingual and multicultural?

But definitely, I've been heavily influenced by the Russian culture of reading, appreciating, and memorizing poetry. I love memorizing and reciting poetry, and used to organize multilingual historical poetry readings as an undergraduate. When I was a graduate student, people for some reason weren't as keen on multilingual poetry readings, although I still frequently participated in Beowulf marathons and Old Norse readings.

You edit Stone Telling, a poetry magazine that managed to publish five poems in its first two issues that were nominated for this year's Rhysling Award, the most prestigious award in the field of speculative poetry. Congratulations! Your very first issue featured a poem by Ursula K. Le Guin, and the list of people who have their poems in issues of ST is really quite impressive. But Rhyslings and famous names aside, why should I come read the poems you publish?

Stone Telling poems talk about things you don't often find elsewhere;

Stone Telling poems address difficult issues, they benefit from multiple rereadings and re-listenings, they are beautiful and full of meaning, and many of them are accompanied by audio recordings and evocative art. We publish newcomers and established poets alike. Try a few, and you'll see what I'm talking about: Shweta Narayan's English/Tamil *Nagapadam* (listen to the recording!), Peer Dudda's heartbreaking English/ASL video poem *Train Go Sorry*, Alexandra Agner's Tertiary, Sonya Taaffe's *Persephone in Hel*, Emily Jiang's Rice *Cooker Dreams*, and Catherynne Valente's *The Secret of Being a Cowboy*, accompanied by a wonderful recording by the musician S. J. Tucker.

What made you publish a poetry magazine in the first place? Why not publish fiction alongside the poems?

Those are two separate questions. I wanted to publish a poetry magazine because I wanted to foreground multi-cultural, boundary-crossing speculative poetry. I felt that there was room for more diversity, more daring, and more serious discourse about speculative poetry, both in our little corner of space-time and around the world. That's why Stone Telling offers non-fiction articles, reviews, and a roundtable alongside the poems. In the process of editing the first three issues, I also discovered that I love reading slush. I'm like a kid in the candy store. Which is why I don't see myself editing fiction; I don't think I would enjoy reading (eating?) fiction slush. In addition, I just don't have the resources to pay decently for fiction.

ST has been a paying market since it first opened shop, but all the content is freely available on the net. Why is that?

As a reader, I want to read wonderful free poetry online. As a poet, I want to be compensated for my work. As an editor, I make the poetry available online for free, and yet do my best to compensate the poets and the columnists for their work. I wish I could pay more, but that would depend on donations, and unfortunately we haven't been receiving many donations.

What is unique about ST? Give me one sentence or one clear image that answers that, please.

It's hard to summarize Stone Telling in one sentence, particularly because my vision of ST and the reality of the issues I put out do not exactly match :) My vision of ST involves showcasing boundary-crossing, innovative, diverse poetry that is daring and unafraid to poke at painful topics. I've done my best to choose diverse, multi-perspective poems that fit this vision, but I'm also a glutton for more.In addition, ST has a combination of words, art, and audio that is, if not exactly unique, at least special enough that people keep commenting about that. I want the magazine to be aesthetically pleasing, and spend a lot of time matching art to poetry. I hope more poets would record mp3s for future issues; it is truly a lovely thing to have.

What influences your decision regarding the rejection or acceptance of a poem for ST?

Since I believe that Stone Telling poems must work on multiple rereadings, I tag all 'maybe' poems and reread them. I must reread a poem at least five times (and love it every time) before committing to buy it. Often I recall lines or images from a particular 'maybe' poem when I am away from my computer (taking a walk, for example, or grading student papers). That's a good indication that a certain piece has become meaningful to me.

I also try to figure out whether the poem works with a particular issue, and with other poems I have accepted for that issue. I still remember - and miss - some poems I have let go because the fit was not right somehow.

What do you want ST to be once that little magazine is properly grown up?

Unforgettable, innovative, inspiring, and thought-provoking.

126

There was this super-important question I forgot to ask--do remind me what it was!

I guess the question is, "What's next for Rose Lemberg?" And the answer is, many new and exciting things! While Shweta Narayan and J. C. Runolfson are guest-editing the fourth issue of Stone Telling, I am busy editing a reprint feminist speculative poetry anthology, The Moment of Change, for Aqueduct Press
(*http://stonetelling.com/change.html*).
Later this summer I will read for the Mythic issue of Stone Telling (ST 5), and after that for the Science and Science Fiction issue (ST 6). I'm writing a YA novel, as I probably mentioned a dozen times, because it's a pretty exciting thing for me. In addition, I'm putting together a poetry collection for a press - cannot give more details yet, but it will be bird-themed.

Then Cried Arthur
by
Peter Chiykowski

This was long before the cup of youth had spilled.
He said he was finished with skewering men
and chasing harts until his horse died under him.
We thought it was wise and kingly to stay in court,
but he wore monarchy like widows wore shawls.
His horse and wife grew restless.

Merlin loved this, of course: Arthur's still heart,
dull ear, yawning mouth, vessels to be filled.
But even the wizard vanished soon thereafter
knowing no Grail could cure people of themselves.
So we ran knights' errands for a couched king
pinned to the throne by the lance of duty.

Perhaps the great death began then,
with him slouching on the drowsy steed of state,
reining lazily, pricking without spurs, drinking
while Lancelot toppled the kingdom with such soft
strokes. The King saw his court stir to scandal.
Still he lay there, crown slumped over brow.

Finally knights of blood and ire came,
and then cried Arthur for horse and armour.
By that late hour his crumpled heart was fit
to drum tantrums more than wars. Mordred put
a sword in him, the river stole him away, but we
who lived know it was the crown that killed him.

The
Wagon Trail

by
John Moran

Herein, a lonely trade...

When the wind had put away its knives and the sky cleared to a black that promised frost, Marcus rose from his post by the Union bank, filled a grey holdall with cardboard bedding, and approached the softly glowing brazier beside the wagon.

"Could I share your fire?" he called from a distance.

"It gives out heat in all directions," its owner replied, lifting his toes to warm the base of his socks. "I see no harm you taking some."

As Marcus approached, the man flapped away a sleeve and shook his hand. He was shorter than he had looked in the day, and his coat flapped as the wind gusted. A loosened tie curled over his high stomach. Beside him stood a pyramid of thirty or forty china cups, glistening in the firelight.

"Horace Runcible," he said.

"I saw you on the wagon, selling drink," Marcus said.

Runcible nodded. "Try some."

He passed over a terracotta jar with a faded label that read, "whiskey," and Marcus took a sip, paused, took another, then passed it back with a frown.

"Tastes like water."

"Some say that. Some do say that."

As Runcible spoke, Marcus noticed the man's eyes travelling up his body and he became conscious of his broken shoes, ill-fitting jacket, and, suddenly, how much his beard itched.

After a moment, Runcible slid nearer -- three o'clock to Marcus's six -- and asked, "how long have you been homeless, son?"

"Four months."

"And how is life?"

"Cold, mostly."

"Have you ever had a job?"

"Yes sir, I've laid sleepers on the railway, and I was once apprenticed to a newspaper."

"So you understand the power of advertising?"

"I guess."

"Take a look at the wagon and tell me what you think of her."

Marcus didn't like to leave the fire, but some resonance in the man's voice made him walk over. When he got there, he rubbed his hand along the wagon's timbers and found them as smooth and hard as pebbles from a stream.

"It's old, isn't it?" he said.

"Been in the family for years," Runcible said, his voice loud above the cracking twigs and ruffling canvas.

Marcus knelt closer. The base planks seemed shapeless in the dark. He made out engravings, smoothed with age, which might have been runes or religious symbols.

Canvas flapped above Marcus' head, and he looked up to see the words, "H. Runcible: Elixir of life."

"Do you like it?" Runcible asked, though from his tone, Marcus wondered if he meant the wagon or something deeper.

"Yeah," he said. "I think I do."

He stumbled back, surprised to find his hands still warm, as if the wood had been heated from within.

Runcible took a long drink, then smiled. "There's a job here, son, if you want it."

"Doing what?"

"Selling water to those who need it, of course."

The next morning, Runcible hitched up two sad-looking horses and they set off.

After a slow beginning, the Kansas countryside began to reveal itself. Traffic whizzed past, but Marcus felt relaxed thanks to a large cooked breakfast. He was also warm for the first time in months.

"Why don't you use a truck?" he asked, as one rumbled past.

"People expect a wagon," Runcible said. "They want the old ways." Then, as the morning turned to afternoon, he added, "Why were you homeless, son?"

"Things didn't work out, I guess."

"You lost your job?"

"Yes sir."

Runcible let the horse plod on for what must have been ten minutes, before asking, "Was it a woman?"

"My wife --" Marcus let the sentence drift off, realising he had no idea how to finish.

"Do you still miss her?"

Marcus laughed. "No." But after a moment, he added, "She took my daughter, Catherine."

"Have this," Runcible said, passing over a jar of elixir.

Ralant took a long drink and looked away.

Soon the wagon began to roll through a thickening row of houses. Runcible parked opposite a row of shops, beside a patch of waste ground.

"Now you'll see the reason for a wagon," he said, tying back the canvas panels.

He leaned out, and held up a bottle, shouting, "people of Kansas, come closer, come closer. This is the elixir of life here. Yes, the elixir of life. Not a drug or a scam -- this is the greatest thing in existence. The actual holy grail in a bottle, better than whiskey and better than beer. Today, you and your family can experience an explosion of satisfaction. Your happiness guaranteed, ladies and gentlemen, or your money back."

To Marcus's amazement, people began to gather, beginning with a couple of pensioners who must have walked over out of nostalgia, but Runcible dealt with each customer in turn, splashing transparent liquid into the mugs Marcus had seen drying the evening before.

Comments spread through the growing crowd. Some twisted their mouth as if the drink tasted bitter, while others took on a faraway look, but most of them asked for more.

"How much?" a short woman asked. She wore a bright red headscarf around greying black hair and clutched a bulging shopping bag.

"One dollar a bottle," Runcible said. "Always has been, always will be."

The woman passed over her money, and Runcible took an empty bottle from the back and filled it from a metal tap that emerged from a dark blue tarpaulin.

Later, when the crowd had departed, they sat watching silvery curtains of rain pour off the canvas, until Marcus said.

"Where does the elixir come from?"

Runcible walked into the back and hauled off the tarpaulin, raising a cloud of dust.

"Rain enters here," he said, pointing to a metal funnel attached to the canvas roof. The funnel led to a dark wood box. "And it's processed here and here." Runcible indicated further boxes in a sequence, all connected by metal tubes. The third was lowest, and held the tap.

"But what's inside the boxes?" Marcus asked.

"Sometimes it's best not to know," Runcible said, and he immediately drew the tarpaulin back, and was unwilling to talk about it further.

Town after town fell like leaves from a tree that had clung on through the winter. In one, Marcus intercepted dregs from a thin bespectacled man who had scrunched up his face as if the drink had been bitter. He sipped it carefully.

"It still tastes like water," he said.

"Some do say that," Runcible said, over his shoulder, as he passed out more to an eager crowd.

Marcus began to help, and served a couple of customers, though he noticed Runcible always handled the money, stuffing dollar after dollar into a dark green satchel on his waist.

Marcus tried calculating the takings. That day alone must have been several hundred dollars, and the next town was no different. Each night Runcible cooked simple food, bought bottles from recycling centres and slept on the floor by the wagon.

Runcible did not move, Marcus realised: he pranced and sprang, twisted and gestured, so that even the black-tee-shirted youths, who Marcus would have thought too proud, had to smile.

In the evening, Marcus watched as Runcible packed the takings bag carefully below his pillow before settling, and imagined how full it had to be. Just three hundred dollars, he thought, might be enough to take him across the state line to see his daughter.

The next town was older, built around a main street with long-established trees. The people wore less clothes here, and they smiled more, though as Marcus calculated their best takings yet, he noticed a boy cross the street with a couple of bottles and share them with three others. The children had ill-fitting clothes, and a thin dog lay beside them, its pale fur even paler along its gaunt stomach.

"Do you ever wonder," Marcus asked that night, "whether we're doing the right thing?"

"We're offering a public service," Runcible said, turning twice to swaddle himself in the dark green blanket he always used.

"Are we?" Marcus said, with such force that Runcible opened his dark eyes and sat up on his elbows.

"What's the problem, son?"

"Just that we're selling rubbish, and then leaving before people find out."

Runcible pointed to the fire, where a small pile of aluminium pots stood stacked after Marcus had washed them. "You weren't complaining when it bought you supper," he said. "Anyway, what do you really mean?"

His eyes seemed to pierce Marcus, and for a moment he felt ashamed, but then he felt the heat of the fire on his cheek, urging him on.

"Just that if we are fleecing suckers, I'd like more out of it." The moment the words were out of his mouth, he felt ashamed, but had no way to take them back.

"Is that so?"

"I mean I'm grateful for you picking me up, but don't you think I deserve a chance to save, and maybe visit my daughter?"

Runcible sat up fully, and for a second Marcus watched his face cross the line of shadow. His nose seemed abnormally long in the darkness.

"You believe we're conning people,"

he said, his voice more resonant than ever, "and because of that you'd like more money?

"Well, I --"

"You want to be a more successful thief, is that it?"

Runcible was louder now, and Marcus found it impossible to look away, but neither could he find words to explain his feelings.

"I have an idea," Runcible said eventually. "We'll be in a new town tomorrow. Why don't you watch me do all the jobs?"

"Marcus felt his breath stop and the night seemed to be at his back close in. He was suddenly conscious of being in a small globe of warmth that did not beat away the cold at all.

"You want to demonstrate you can do without me," he said, and even to him his voice sounded desperate.

"Not exactly, " Runcible said. "I want you to learn."

The next morning, as they dropped down to the town, the only sound a jingle of harness and the slow whoosh of a car, Runcible said, "tell me about your daughter."

"She's thin, with brown hair," Marcus said.

"What does she want to do with her life."

"I don't know."

"Does she have any hobbies?"

"Drawing maybe."

"What's her favourite flower?"

"Jesus, Runcible, she's just a little girl."

"Did you never try talking to her?"

For a moment Marcus had a lump in his throat, and Runcible must have noticed, because he passed over some elixir as easily as he offered it to a customer.

Marcus stared at the grey horizon first.

"Maybe not enough," he said eventually, "but it wasn't right to take her away, either." He drank then, without looking over at Runcible, and when he finished he realised that the water had tasted sweeter than usual. It seemed more filling, too, as if he were a dried-up sponge struggling to regain its shape.

That morning, Marcus watched as Runcible said to one woman, "Just think, madam, with this drink, dresses as beautiful as the one you wear now will be bought for you always," then to a man whose body sagged inside his beige tee shirt and slacks, he knelt and whispered, "this, sir, is health for the body as well as the mind."

Runcible did not move, Marcus realised: he pranced and sprang, twisted and gestured, so that even the black-tee-shirted youths, who Marcus would have thought too proud, had to smile.

136

And wherever Runcible went, people bought and bought.

Halfway through, as Marcus had learned to time the ebb and flow of crowds, Runicible stepped back and asked, "were you watching me, or them?"

"You, I guess,"

"Then watch them instead. This is your chance."

He strode forward again, and this time Marcus followed a young man in a faded suit worn to a shine over his right shoulder. The man hovered on the edge of the crowd, leaving Marcus unsure whether he was wary of buying or nervous of people, but when, suddenly, the queue thinned, the man advanced and spoke with a shaking high voice.

"May I have some."

Runcible knelt, and said, "not from me," so loudly that Marcus stared in astonishment, but before he could turn away, Runcible placed a hand on his shoulder and said, "but please allow my assistant to help you."

The man stepped to the side, but as Marcus filled a bottle with the translucent liquid, he still could not understand why anyone should buy it.

He sealed it with a cork and passed it over, then, because he did not want to take advantage of the man, he also poured him a small cupful.

"Try this first," he said.

The man coughed so deeply, that after a dozen seconds, Marcus wondered if it might turn him inside out, but he slowly regained his poise and took the water as if it was precious. He drained it, and for the first time, smiled.

"Yes," he said. "That's how I remember it."

He bought two more bottles, and as he walked away, Marcus watched him swing them against his leg, as if listening to music.

Am I the only one who can't taste it? Marcus wondered.

That night, he waited till Runcible finished spooning sausages from the casserole - and then said, "I watched that man seem to change after tasting the elixir. Is that what you wanted me to see?"

"Maybe."

"What's in it?"

"What do you think?"

Marcus took a sip from the cup he had poured himself, wondering if repeated attempts were making him more sensitive or more gullible. It still tasted of water, although soft, too, as if the rain had dripped every piece of hardness out. If you added soap, the lather would never stop, Marcus thought.

"Oak casks make wine taste different," he said after running it over his tongue for a long time. "Is that what people taste?"

Runcible smiled. "Ever heard of the placebo effect, son?"

"Where a drug works because everyone believes in it."

Runcible nodded, then leaned back against the wagon and closed his eyes till he appeared to be asleep. "Sometimes it's best not to know," he said at last.

Marcus found the evening quiet after that. Runcible seemed disinclined to talk, so he watched the fire dance through the holes in the brazier, and felt its warmth sink sweetly into his bones. He yawned and stretched, feeling at peace, though he knew he'd have to move on sooner rather than later. Ever since he'd joined, he'd felt his daughter growing ever more distant, and this was no way of earning the money to see her on equal terms.

Just as he was wrapping himself in his blanket, Runcible whispered, "I've been waiting for you to taste it, but I think you're near enough."

"For what?"

Runcible stretched out under his own blanket, staring upwards. Marcus followed his gaze, then smiled at the high white clouds and the crescent moon.

"I've not been a good man," Runcible said.

"I don't --"

"-- because I've been weak. My problem was whiskey."

"But you only ever drink elixir?"

Runcible whispered something that sounded like "hmh," then added, "what do you call a man who drinks only water, son?"

"A teetotaller?"

"An alcoholic."

"I don't think any of us are without sin, sir."

Runcible did not reply, and Marcus watched the clouds slide past and wondered how he would fare on the day of judgement. 'Your crime is indifference and anger,' he imagined the heavenly lord saying.

By the time he thought of another reply, Runcible was snoring, so he let himself drift into sleep too.

When he woke, he was alone -- and when he pulled on his clothes and walked round the wagon, he found nothing but two horses cropping the grass, and a small letter upon the riding seat.

Dear Marcus,

I suppose it's time when it feels time. Here's a secret no-one knows: I've been an actor, a singer and a politician, but selling this elixir has felt like the only honest thing I've done.

I inherited the wagon from a pair of fellows in Missouri, who got it from a woman further south, and she got it from someone before that. If you look at the construction you'll see it's older

138

than any of us, and now it's yours.

There are only two things you don't know that you ought - one is the best route, which I've drawn on the back of this letter like they did for me, and the other's that you should never look into the boxes. Sometimes it's best not to know, son.

Other than that, just learn to love her like I did, keep the horses fed, and in any case I'm not giving you much choice because I'm keeping the money. I wanted capital to retire with, and when I took you on I already had enough. I've known for many a town that it was time to move on.

Look me up if you're in Bellingham sometime,

Your friend,

Horace Runcible

P.S. What with the name already painted on the side, it'd be good business sense for you to begin calling yourself that. It worked better for me than my own, Russell Philip Stanmore.

Marcus walked into town and checked the railway and greyhound stations, but Runcible had gone.

When he returned to the wagon he found Runcible's cup and sleeping blanket neatly stacked inside with the dark green money pouch, though, as promised, the pouch was empty.

The next two towns were lonely. Marcus took over three hundred dollars in the first and four hundred in the second, but he kept missing Runcible. Rather than squandering money on hotel rooms, he kept to the life he had been shown, making a fire each night and sleeping by the wagon, though each morning he woke early and stared across the cold brazier as if the old man might be still lying there.

Part-way through the third day, Marcus went in search of a bank.

"Can I help you sir," said the teller with a smile, that made Marcus feel uncomfortable even though he knew he was clean from a standing wash. Nonetheless, he placed the dark green bag onto the counter, smiled, and said, "I'd like to open a deposit account with six hundred dollars."

It was the same situation in town after town. He bathed in rivers when he could and banked money without checking the balance. When the rain grew scarce, he filled the funnel with tap-water, and still couldn't notice a difference.

He got into a rhythm and managed for a time to forget Runcible, and even Catherine. Occasionally, he pulled back the tarpaulin and stared at the dark wood boxes, but he always obeyed Runcible's advice and left them alone.

One night, six months later, Marcus was passing a pawn shop when something caught his eye. It was a tiny ring for a child's fingers, and he almost wept as he imagined how much larger Catherine now had to be.

He returned to the bank and asked how much was in his account. The answer elated and terrified him in equal measure.

When Marcus returned that evening, he brushed down the horses and stared at the city lights on the horizon.

"This is better than being homeless," he said to no-one in particular, adding, "I need a bit more to be certain."

That night, he thought he imagined Runcible's voice on the wind, calling him a coward.

The next town was prosperous, as was the one after that. And though a few customers complained that the elixir was just water, there were no more than usual. Yet he had a feeling, as the days grew cooler, and the rain glazed the slowly plodding horses, that he was a slow fuse heading for a moment of explosion.

One night, he brought the wagon away and caught a glimpse of men standing beside a tree. Although there was a streetlight opposite, they had chosen to stand in the shadows.

As he drew closer they approached, and Marcus saw that their clothes weren't good and one's trainers had a split down the side. He stared at their faces and wondered what to say, because they seemed so very young.

He nodded to the first boy, who had to be in his early twenties.

"Can I help?"

"We want your money," the boy said, his hand shaking as he took out a knife.

Marcus glanced at the other, who was walking to the far side of the wagon. His first thought was, that they were stealing from his daughter's future, and he began to grow angry -- the kind of anger that had stormed him out of the house when he had been married.

As they approached, Marcus grabbed a long metal soup ladle. For some reason, the boys became entwined with Catherine in his mind. He imagined her lying on the pavement somewhere, attacked by thugs like these and his anger grew still more. He had worked too hard, he thought, to be robbed.

As the first boy put his hand onto the side of the wagon, Marcus swung the ladle and felt it connect. The boy vanished onto the wet road, and without waiting, Marcus swung the ladle at the second boy and hit him in the face.

He leapt from the wagon, but the fight had gone. One boy had blood across his nose and the other held his arm as if it was broken.

Marcus advanced and they backed

off, then collapsed as their backs touched the wagon, sliding down to the floor. The boy holding his arm whispered, "please, mister, don't hurt us."

Marcus felt his anger collapse, too.

"You're just kids," he said. "How old are you?"

"Twenty-three, mister, and my brother's twenty-two."

Marcus's ladle slipped lower until it came to rest against his thigh. He looked at the plastic bags lining their shoes, and remembered how he had felt once.

"You're homeless," he said. It wasn't a question.

"We got a home if we want."

"But you don't, do you?"

The boy looked away. "We need to get out of town."

As Marcus knelt, the boy flinched. "Was it your daddy beat you?" he asked.

"Yes sir."

Despite his temper, that was the one thing he had never done to Catherine. Marcus felt furious again, though this time cold and determined and focused on the boy's father.

He reached out and took the boy's arm, feeling along it. "I don't think it's broken," he said at last.

"I'm sorry," the boy said.

Marcus nodded, noticing how both boys gripped the base timbers, as if the ancient wood gave them comfort, and he wondered just how long the wagon had been plying its lonely trade and how many drivers it had helped. Above the boys, behind the driver's seat and past the rows of stacked up bottles were a set of wooden boxes he had never looked into, and now he realised he never would.

He smiled, realising he had kept the trust Runcible had implied, but never fully explained. If he had looked, he wondered whether he might have seen something to prevent him from honestly passing the wagon on. In the distance, he thought he felt Runcible smiling.

Marcus stepped back and looked down at the boys, though his mind was filled with his daughter and what it might be like to see her once more.

"The name's Horace Runcible," he said, "and I offer you food and a ride to the next town if you'll have it. Work, too, if you want."

When he held out his hand, the boy with the bust nose sniffed once and blinked, then took it.

———————————————

Contributors...

Therese Arkenberg

Therese Arkenberg is a student from Wisconsin. On the rare instances where she puts down her pen, she can be found reading a book (more often a textbook than not these days) or making yet another attempt to organize her desk and her collection of stuffed animals. She has fiction published or forthcoming from Beneath Ceaseless Skies and the anthologies All About Eve, Things We Are Not, Thoughtcrime Experiments, Warrior Wisewoman 3, and Sword and Sorceress XXIV. Her novella, Aqua Vitae, has been accepted by WolfSinger Publications for a 2011 release.

Several of her short stories are also available at AnthologyBuilder.com.

Website: mumblingsage.tumblr.com

Blog: mumblingsage.livejournal.com

Twitter: @TArkenberg

Luis Beltrán

Luis Beltrán tells the stories of his daydreams through his latest body of digital print photographs. These quietly seductive works hold a deep and moving quality of innocent desire. Figures appear at the ends of alleys, above cityscapes, and up trees; they draw you towards them, making the eye chase its new companion. Beltrán's photos produce a dreamlike sensation, the product of their deeply saturated, yet muted, coloration. While objects around the periphery of the central image maintain a luscious intensity with their dark shadows and full mid-tones, the focus shifts as the eyes finds a hazy subconscious perspective. The figures which are central to this misty state call feelingly to the viewer. Beltrán has created a world that captures a sense of the 'other,' and speaks to the mind's natural curiosity. His photos call to a place within us all and echo the inner child's adventurous and courageous nature. Luis Beltrán was born in Spain and still lives there, in Valencia.

www.luisbeltran.es

Chelsea Brandt

Chelsea Brandt is a young artist preparing to depart home for university this year. Her work has been recognized in the Texas Art Education Association VASE 2011 with a 4 rating (superior), the highest available. She also received an honorable mention in the 2010-2011 Texas PTA Reflections program.

Peter Chiykowski

Peter Chiykowski lives and schemes in Halifax, Nova Scotia. His writing has been published (or is forthcoming from) The New Quarterly, Grain, OnSpec, and Basement Stories. His comic, Rock, Paper, Cynic, can be found in university newspapers across eastern Canada and online at:

www.rockpapercynic.com and www.littleworlds.ca

Lawrence Conquest

Lawrence Conquest is a British author who has had short stories published in various magazines and anthologies, including Black Static and Sick Things. He has also written comic strips for FutureQuake Press and an audio story for the BBC's Doctor Who.

www.lawrence-conquest.blogspot.com

M. S. Corley

M. S. Corley is a freelance illustrator and graphic designer who is strongly influenced by literature and the past. He currently lives in Washington with his wife and cat named Dinah.

http://www.mscorley.blogspot.com/
http://www.flickr.com/photos/mscorley/
http://mscorley.deviantart.com/gallery/

Jude-Marie Green

Jude-Marie Green has sold a few stories here and there (M-Brane, ElectricSpec, Jack O'Spec, most recently) after a lifetime of reading the classics: Jules Verne, Edgar Allan Poe, and Miguel de Cervantes. She graduated from Clarion West in 2010 and is currently editor at 10Flash Magazine and e2MPi. She lives in Southern California and dreams of motorcycles.

10Flash: http://www.10flash.wordpress.com
e2MPi: http://www.radio-sf.com/home/fanzines/e2pmi-zine
http://judemariegreen.wikispaces.com

Mari Kurisato

Mari Kurisato is a 34 year old recovering hikikomori digital illustrator, Twitter addict, and unpublished novelist, working on her fourth novel. She lives at home with her infant son, wife, mom and cat somewhere in the US. She has an irrational crush on Masamune Shirow, and considers Elizabeth Moon her personal deity. Despite her pen name, she is not Japanese. Her website can be found at:

http://www.marikurisato.com
@MariKurisato
www.facebook.com/marikurisato

Simone Martel

Simone Martel is the author of a book of creative nonfiction, The Expectant Gardener. Her shorter nonfiction has appeared in Greenprints and other magazines. Her stories have appeared in The Long Story, Short Story Review, Fogged Clarity and Magnolia Review. She has a BA in English from U.C. Berkeley and lives in Berkeley with her husband and teenage son.

Simone Martel is an author on LibraryThing and Red Room.

John Moran

John Moran graduated with a degree in Physics some time ago, and has been grappling with the nature of the universe ever since. He has worked as a nuclear physicist, computer programmer and information security consultant as well as being the owner of an art shop.

John has had one story published in Flash Fiction online, and has another forthcoming in Nature Magazine.

He lives near Manchester, England, with his wife.

Michael A. Pignatella

Michael Pignatella lives in Connecticut with his wife and two children. His short fiction has appeared in such venues as Tales of the Unanticipated, Sounds of the Night, Murky Depths, Wicked Hollow, Aiofe's Kiss, Dark Corners, nanobison, Modern Magic, All Possible Worlds, Withersin, and Wondrous Web Worlds vol. 4. His story "Remember the Face of Your Son," which appeared in Withersin, Birth:1 received an Honorable Mention in The Year's Best Fantasy and Horror 2008. He is currently shopping a novel while he works on producing yet another.

Blog:
http://dispassionatewitness.wordpress.com

William C. Rasmussen

William "Bill" Rasmussen began writing horror fiction back in 1985, and from that point until early 1991 had almost 100 short stories published in the small press. He stepped away from the keyboard until early 2010, due to occupational priorities and familial responsibilities. He retired from the Federal Government in 2004, and in March of 2010, resumed his passion for writing horror stories. His collection CLAW MARKS & OTHER DISTURBING DIVERSIONS was released in digital format in September, 2010, by Crossroad Press, and is available at Amazon.com. He has short fiction upcoming in Sounds of the Night #8 and

Black Ink Horror #8. He resides comfortably with his loving wife in Cordova, TN.

Edward W. Robertson

Ed's fiction is upcoming at AE: The Canadian Science Fiction Review and can be found in M-Brane SF and Reflection's Edge, among other places. He recently moved to LA, where in addition to writing fiction, he works as a movie critic and freelancer. If he could find a way to get paid for walking around on the beach, he'd be set for life. Ed blogs at

http://edwardwrobertson.blogspot.com/

Jeremy Schliewe

Jeremy Schliewe lives and writes in Tucson, Arizona.

Alexandra Seidel

Alexandra Seidel does not believe in either talking swords or pink elephants. In spite of this obvious limitation, she writes prose and poetry, often--though not exclusively--about the fantastical, and occasionally, some of it gets published: Sybil's Garage, Electric Velocipede, Beyond Centauri, Labyrinth Inhabitant Magazine and others.

Every once or twice, Alexandra blogs. She is never quite sure about what.

Better go see for yourself:

http://tigerinthematchstickbox.blogspot.com/
http://twitter.com/Alexa Seidel
http://www.facebook.com/alexa.seidel

Magen Toole

Magen Toole is an author based in Fort Worth, Texas. She likes dinosaurs and black holes, and when she grows up she wants to play tambourine in a psychedelic revival band.

Website address http://www.eonism.net

Publisher's Note...

The shared world of The Aether Age has been one of the most gratifying things I have been involved with, and I am delighted to see it spotlighted here. Creative collaboration is a lot of fun, but I don't think I knew how satisfying it could be before I saw the Aether Age universe take shape, so many fascinating elements of its history, cultures, and physical laws emanating from the creative minds of many different writers who read our general premise for it and made it their own.

As the contents of the original book were selected, it was exciting and sometimes startling how neatly the stories began to fit together considering that each person who wrote one of those stories was working without any knowledge of what anyone else was doing. But now that the original set of stories is out there in the form of that lovely book, we have reached the point where we can see the start of something just as cool as the initial collaboration: the cross-pollination of ideas, the building upon the concept, the elaboration upon concepts and themes from the first group of stories.

This issue features Edward W. Robertson's new Aether Age story, in which he picks up once again with the characters and situations of his story from the anthology, "The Inspiration of Philocrates." But Robertson's new item is not just a sequel to his own story. While it builds upon his own work, it also gathers together background elements and terminology introduced by other writers in the anthology. This is exactly what Brandon and I had hoped would happen, the creation of more new stories that would further enrich and interconnect the shared world.

We hope that readers who like thoughtful speculative fiction and alternate history and who have not yet read The Aether Age will do so immediately. A short summary of the concept might make some readers assume that it's just another twist on steampunk and make them pass it by if they have already had their fill of the trappings of that subgenre. Even though the founding question of the Aether Age premise—what if mass literacy had happened thousands of years earlier than it did in our world?—is somewhat like steampunk speculations, our project has resulted in a very different, unexpected world.

Writers who find the concept appealing are in luck because the Aether Age's Creative Commons license makes it available to anyone who wants to write new stories in its world or create any other kind of media based upon it, adding to the great collaboration that has the Aether Age has been so far and which continues here in the new edition of Fantastique Unfettered.

—Christopher Fletcher, M-Brane Press

(/Unless)